Books in The Nancy Drew Files® Series

THE
NANCY DREW
FILES™

Case 66

TALL, DARK
AND DEADLY

CAROLYN KEENE

AN ARCHWAY PAPERBACK
Published by POCKET BOOKS
New York   London   Toronto   Sydney   Tokyo   Singapore

AN ARCHWAY PAPERBACK *Original*

An Archway Paperback published by
POCKET BOOKS, a division of Simon & Schuster Inc.
1230 Avenue of the Americas, New York, NY 10020

Copyright © 1991 by Simon & Schuster Inc.
Produced by Mega-Books of New York, Inc.

ISBN: 0-671-73070-3

First Archway Paperback printing December 1991

10 9 8 7 6 5 4 3 2

NANCY DREW, AN ARCHWAY PAPERBACK and colophon are registered trademarks of Simon & Schuster Inc.

THE NANCY DREW FILES is a trademark of Simon & Schuster Inc.

Cover art by Tom Galasinski

Printed in the U.S.A.

IL 6+

Chapter

One

"TURN UP THE VOLUME, Bess," Nancy Drew said, drumming her hands on the steering wheel. "This is my favorite song."

Bess Marvin tapped her foot to the beat as she twisted the knob on the car stereo. "You know what this feels like, Nancy?" she asked. "Remember going back to school at the end of the summer? Getting ready to study hard . . ."

Nancy laughed and leaned back against the seat to stretch her shoulders. Sunlight danced through her red-gold hair as she turned to look at her friend. "Bess," she teased, "it's the middle of winter. And we're going to school to investigate, not study."

1

"You never know," Bess said airily. "You can always learn something."

"Well, maybe we'll learn that Ava Woods just took off for a long weekend, and now she's back safe and sound, and we can go to Florida as we planned."

Bess's blue eyes opened in surprise. "I thought we were off to save a desperate girl spirited away by her blind date. You mean she may not be missing? And I gave up a Florida tan for her?"

"Bess, what's happened to your sense of adventure? I told you everything I know. Ava went on a blind date Friday night. She didn't come back Saturday or yesterday. She may have had plans for the weekend that she didn't tell anyone about, and she could be on her way back now."

"Or maybe she fell in love at first sight and eloped," Bess suggested.

"Maybe," Nancy agreed. "Here's the exit for Halloway College. We're about to find out."

Halloway College was a sprawling Gothic campus about an hour from River Heights. Nancy and Bess drove in through the main entrance and asked the guard on duty how to get to the administration building. As Nancy steered her Mustang along the meandering campus road, Bess turned her eyes toward their surroundings. "Nice place," she commented.

"Mm-hmm. Looks a little like Ned's campus." Ned was Nancy's longtime boyfriend, who attended Emerson College. Nancy pulled into the parking lot in front of a gray stone building. "Let's go."

Nancy and Bess were directed to Dean Selig, Halloway's dean of students, who was expecting them. He was a short, pudgy man who looked lost behind a huge black desk. As he jumped up to greet them, he smoothed down the few wisps of hair on his mostly bald head. His gray eyes smiled from behind round glasses as he invited the girls to sit down.

"You're Ava's friend Nancy Drew," he began.

Nancy introduced Bess and then corrected the dean. "I've never actually met Ava," she explained. "Mr. and Mrs. Woods are friends of my father, and they asked me to help find her."

Dean Selig looked disturbed. "I wish they would notify the police," he said, shaking his head. "Please don't be offended—I trust your abilities, Nancy—but you can never be too careful."

"Well, Ava's been gone only for the weekend," Nancy said. "She could come back any minute. Does the school have a policy about notifying the police?"

"No." The dean shrugged. "That's why I haven't pushed them. Students are responsible for themselves. They have to attend a certain number of classes in order to take their exams, but even that isn't absolute."

"According to Mrs. Woods, Ava's roommate doesn't know where she is," Nancy explained. "I

3

wanted to talk to some of her other friends to see if she told anyone where she was going. But I'd like to keep things quiet, if it's possible."

"Quiet?" Dean Selig looked puzzled.

"Well, we aren't sure this is a case of foul play. If Ava just forgot to tell anyone where she was going, she'll be pretty embarrassed if I tell everyone she's missing. And if something serious did happen, we don't want the person responsible to know we're investigating."

"So you want to go undercover," the dean said, pressing a button on his phone with one pudgy finger. "You're in luck. We're just starting our January-term optional program of nonacademic study. We offer it every winter."

"Nonacademic study?" Bess looked puzzled.

"The classes are very general, but the students get the flavor of a subject they're interested in. Registration began on Thursday, so most of the classes will probably be full," the dean continued. "But I'll enroll you both as students and assign you rooms in the dorms. There's plenty of space. The school is only about half full."

The dean's secretary appeared in the doorway, and soon Nancy and Bess were enrolled as transfer students. Nancy asked about the size of the student body and found out that seven hundred students were enrolled for the winter term. She and Bess would have to split up to cover enough ground, she realized. She asked for two separate rooms in Ava's dorm so no one would connect her with Bess.

Dean Selig hovered nearby as they had their pictures taken for student ID cards. When he asked if there was anything else he could do, Nancy assured him she would call him the moment she needed help. After Nancy picked up a parking sticker for her car, she and Bess headed over to the gym to register for classes.

The campus buildings were scattered among lawns and small hills. Stark, leafless trees stood out against a snowy background. When Nancy and Bess reached the gymnasium, where registration was taking place, they were dismayed to find a line of students stretching out the door.

"Why don't I stay here and register for both of us?" Bess suggested. "You can take our stuff over to the dorm and get settled."

Nancy looked at her in surprise. "I don't believe you're offering to stand here in the snow," she said. "Is there a cute guy in the line I missed?"

Bess smiled. "This will be a good way to meet people," she said. "Besides, with your brain, you'd probably sign us up for calculus or something. I want to pick my own course."

Nancy drove to Hartley Hall, the dorm that Ava Woods lived in. Dragging the suitcases into the lobby, she thought that Bess had packed enough clothes for a year, as usual. The girl at the front desk gave her directions to the head resident's room. Leaving the bags in the lobby, she went to introduce herself and pick up her keys.

The head resident was a senior named Maura Parker, who had green eyes and a mass of curly black hair. As she looked for Nancy's keys, she went over the rules of the dorm. According to Maura, the door was locked promptly at midnight and could be opened only with a card key. Hartley had one main phone number, with an extension on each floor for incoming calls. There was a loudspeaker system to let people know when they had calls.

"It's not too bad, except at the beginning of the term," Maura assured her. "After a few weeks, most students have phones installed in their rooms."

Nancy thanked Maura and took her bags up to her room, leaving Bess's by the reception desk. "They belong to someone I met at registration," she explained to the girl on duty. "I had a car, so I said I'd bring them by for her."

Nancy's room was on the third floor, right next to Ava's. It was small and bare. A narrow bed stood under the only window, and a desk and dresser leaned on the opposite wall.

Quickly she unpacked her jeans and sweaters, then took out the two dresses she had brought and hung them in the closet. She debated whether to wait for Bess, then decided not to waste any time. Grabbing a notebook out of her purse, she went next door.

An attractive young woman in a dancer's leotard answered Nancy's knock.

"I'm looking for Betsy Campbell," Nancy said.

"You found her," the girl said. "You must be Nancy Drew." She moved out of the way to let Nancy pass. "Mrs. Woods told me you were coming."

Nancy looked around for a place to sit. The room was larger than her own, with two beds, desks, and dressers. Nancy guessed Betsy's side of the room was the one with the poster of a dancer above the bed. She sat in the desk chair on the other side.

"Mrs. Woods gave me your name," Nancy explained. "She said you were the one who reported Ava missing."

Betsy blushed. "It wasn't exactly what I meant to do. I hope I haven't gotten her into trouble."

"I don't see how," Nancy said encouragingly. "We're all just interested in making sure she's okay." She gestured to her notebook. "Do you mind if I take notes? It helps me remember."

Betsy shook her head and waited for Nancy to get a pen. "I woke up on Saturday and saw that Ava wasn't here," she began when Nancy was settled. "I just assumed she'd gone home for the weekend without telling me. She only lives about ten miles away, so she goes home fairly often.

7

Then she got a couple of phone calls, so I tried to reach her. It wasn't until I spoke to Mrs. Woods that I found out she hadn't gone home."

"And you don't know where she might be?"

Betsy shook her head. "Mrs. Woods asked me if I knew who Ava's Friday-night date was, but I don't. I just know it was a blind date."

Nancy picked up a large, silver-framed photograph that was sitting on the desk. Betsy was in it, her dark skin and hair contrasting with that of the pretty girl she hugged. "Is this Ava?" Nancy asked, pointing to the girl with long wavy blond hair and brown eyes.

Betsy nodded.

"Do you think I could have a picture of her?"

"Do you want that one?" Betsy asked doubtfully.

"No." Nancy smiled. "Something a little smaller would be good."

Nancy moved out of the way as Betsy began rummaging through Ava's desk drawer.

"Here's her extra student ID," Betsy offered finally. "She lost it for a while, so she has two. Would that help?"

Nancy took the ID and looked at the small photo. "This is fine," she said, slipping it into her purse. "Now tell me what Ava's like—her hobbies, interests, anything that might have drawn her away over the weekend."

As Betsy spoke, a picture of Ava emerged. She

was funny, impulsive, and very well liked. She loved sports and adventure. She had a few good friends, but most of them were away during the winter term. A sophomore, she was an economics major. In her spare time she worked for a program in town called Elderly Assistance.

"She doesn't sound like someone who would need help to get a date," Nancy commented. "She doesn't have a steady boyfriend, then?"

"Not at the moment," Betsy said.

"Tell me about her Friday-night blind date," Nancy suggested. "Whatever you remember."

"I don't think she was very excited about it," Betsy said, uncrossing her slender legs as she leaned toward Nancy. "She was tired and wanted to cancel, but I pushed her to go. It was the night of the Winter Welcome Dance, and I invited her and her date to go with me, but she kept saying she didn't want to."

"So she and her date didn't go to the dance?"

"No, I would have seen them," Betsy said. "She grabbed her car keys on the way out and said she had to pick Jim up. I guess that was her date's name. Apparently he lived off campus, and his car had broken down. I don't know where they were going."

"And she never came back from the date, as far as you know," Nancy mused. "Are her keys around?"

Betsy shook her head. "No, I checked. By

yesterday I was nervous. I even walked around campus looking for her car. It's not where she usually parks it, and I haven't seen it anywhere else, either."

"Is there some record of cars on campus?" Nancy asked.

"I don't think so. They give you a parking sticker if you're a student, and that's it."

"Right," Nancy said. "Now, who arranged the date?"

"There's a student-run dating service called Campus Connections," Betsy told her. "A lot of students use it. They match couples on the computer according to their interests."

"Who runs it?"

"A senior named Luke Jefferies. I think he has a couple of people who help out."

"Is it sponsored by the school?" Nancy said, wondering if the dean could get her more information.

"I'm not sure," Betsy said.

"Can you think of anything else that might help me?"

Betsy frowned and shook her head. "I'll let you know if something occurs to me," she promised.

"What about the phone calls you mentioned?" Nancy asked. "Could one of them have been from this Jim?"

"No, they were from a woman. Now that you mention it, though, they were very strange calls.

The woman wouldn't tell me her name. She just kept saying Ava must call her immediately. And she said something about a box."

"Can you remember exactly what she said?" Nancy asked.

Betsy shook her head in frustration. "She wasn't making much sense. She kept saying Ava would know. And she said Ava had her box, or she needed to know about her box, or something."

"An old voice, a young voice?" Nancy prodded. "Do you remember an accent or anything?"

"An older voice," Betsy said slowly. "The woman sounded upset. I thought at the time it was one of Ava's teachers or maybe a family friend, but I didn't really worry about it."

Nancy closed her notebook. "I'm next door in room three-fourteen, if you remember anything else or if you hear anything. Can you point me toward Campus Connections? They may be able to help."

Betsy told her the dating service was on the north end of the campus and gave her directions for a shortcut.

On her way out of the room, Nancy stopped. "I don't know what the Woodses said to you, but they asked me to keep Ava's disappearance quiet as long as possible," she began.

"Oh, I won't say a word," Betsy assured her quickly. "I feel bad enough as it is."

Nancy looked sharply at Betsy. "Bad? Why?"

"Well, Ava's parents did find out from me that she was gone."

"But you didn't have anything to do with her disappearance, right?" Nancy prompted.

"Of course not!"

"Then don't blame yourself," Nancy said.

As she went back to her room to change, Nancy thought about Betsy's reaction. The girl seemed concerned about the fact that she'd told the Woodses Ava was missing. Why would Betsy want to keep quiet about Ava's disappearance? Talking to Ava's other friends might shed some light on Betsy's attitude.

Nancy grabbed a turquoise sweater from her suitcase and slipped her boots on. When she got downstairs she saw that Bess's bags were still in the lobby. She dashed off a note to tell Bess where she was going and slipped it under the handle of one suitcase.

Betsy's directions took Nancy across the field she had seen from her window. There had been a snowstorm the previous evening, and the field was a pure white expanse, sparkling in the sunlight. The campus seemed deserted. No one had taken Nancy's path across the field. As her boots crunched in the snow, Nancy almost felt bad about the footprints she was leaving behind.

She strolled along, collecting her thoughts. How much should she tell the people at Campus Connections? she wondered. If someone there was responsible for Ava's disappearance, Nancy didn't want that person to know she was investigating. And how did the phone calls from the woman fit into the picture?

Nancy heard fast footsteps and a male voice behind her. "Hey, you!" the voice growled.

She began to turn. Out of the corner of her eye she saw a dark figure wind up and hurl something at her.

Too late Nancy tried to duck. An explosion of cold hit her full in the face. Then she fell backward into the snow!

Chapter

Two

Nancy gasped and rubbed her face, struggling to sit up. She opened her eyes to see a handsome, dark-skinned guy bending toward her. His face flushed as he saw her expression.

"Oh, excuse me," he said, trying to help her up. "I don't know you! I mean, I thought you were someone else."

"Someone you don't like, obviously," Nancy said wryly, brushing herself off.

"I'm terribly sorry," he said, sounding sincere. "I wasn't aiming for your head. I wasn't even aiming for you! It's a silly game that I play with a friend. Please forgive me."

"Well, my jeans are soaked, but no broken

bones," Nancy said. "I suppose I can forgive you."

The stranger's face broke into an attractive smile. "Darien Olivares at your service, beautiful stranger," he said, sticking his hand out.

Nancy grinned and introduced herself. "You certainly have an odd way of meeting women," she teased. "Most of the guys I know stopped hitting girls to get their attention in first grade."

Darien fell into step beside her. "May I escort you to your destination?" he asked.

"Actually, no, don't bother," Nancy said. "I'm just going to Campus Connections."

"You're looking for a date?" he asked. "Nancy Drew, your search is over. I'll take you wherever you wish to go."

Nancy smiled and shook her head. "That's very kind, but no thank you. I prefer to go to Campus Connections."

Darien feigned sadness. "Are you a student here?" he asked.

"For the January session," Nancy said.

"Then you can get to know me," he said. "And maybe you'll change your mind."

"Maybe," Nancy said as they came to the building Darien had pointed out. "Now, if you don't mind . . ."

"I'll leave you here," Darien said, taking the hint. "But promise you won't forget me."

How could I? Nancy thought, smiling.

Seeing no guard in the building, she checked the directory and climbed the stairs to the third floor. She rang the buzzer for room 303. After a moment she saw a shadow through the frosted pane in the door. A lanky guy with long, sandy hair answered the door.

"Hi, it's usually open," he said, letting her in. "You're new, aren't you?" After Nancy introduced herself, he said, "I'm Luke Jefferies. Sit down. I'll be back in a minute."

Nancy sat in the small lobby while Luke hurried into an office and brought back a clipboard with a form attached. "Fill this out while you're waiting," he directed, before running back into the office and closing the door behind him.

Nancy looked at the papers he'd handed her. "You and Your Dream Date," the title read. It was a questionnaire for the dating service, she realized. She flipped through it, smiling at such questions as "Is your ideal date a moonlit walk on the beach or an expensive night on the town?" At the back of the questionnaire there were pages to "evaluate your connection" and record the success or failure of your date.

Nancy waited for a few minutes. When Luke didn't return she knocked on his door.

"Done already?" he asked when he opened the door.

"Actually, no," Nancy said. "I'm not sure I want to use your service. I need some more information first."

Luke sat down behind his desk. "Don't worry, everything's confidential. You pay fifteen dollars to enroll, and you get seven dates free."

"How do you screen clients?" Nancy asked.

"If you're a student, that's all you need," Luke said. "I don't discriminate. After all, one person's nerd may be someone else's prince."

"So how exactly do you arrange a date?"

"Well, you ask for one, first of all, and tell me what day you need the date for. Then the computer matches you up with the perfect person. I check the day and time with him and arrange for him to pick you up at the appointed time. And of course I give you his name and phone number in case something happens."

"Do you keep records of every date?"

"Yes, why?" Luke wrinkled his forehead.

"Well, I'm just trying to get a feel for the service. You run it, right?" Nancy asked.

Luke nodded. "It was my idea, and it's my service. It's a great success, if I do say so myself. I hope you're not planning to copy it."

"No," Nancy assured him. "I just want to know, for example, what will happen to this questionnaire once I fill it out."

Luke gave her a measuring look. "It will go into your file, along with your evaluations, the records of all the dates you agree to, and whatever else is important. Now it's your turn to answer a question. Why all the curiosity?"

"Actually, I'm hoping you can give me some

information about someone who used your service," Nancy said. "Can you tell me anything about Ava Woods's date on Friday night?"

Luke looked startled. "Ava . . . Ava Woods." He shuffled some papers on his desk. "I don't carry all this information around in my head, you know," he snapped, flustered. "She's not a regular."

"Couldn't you check your files?" Nancy asked. "All I need is her date's name."

"Sorry, I can't," Luke said, regaining his smooth manner. "It's confidential."

"This is important," Nancy urged. "Couldn't you bend a rule this once?"

"Tell me why you need to know."

Nancy sighed. "I'm afraid I can't do that right now," she said.

"You have a lot of questions and no answers," Luke said. "Why don't you ask Ava Woods?"

"I can't do that, either," Nancy said. She studied Luke for a moment, trying to decide how much she should tell him. "She's . . . not here."

Luke shrugged. "Wait till she comes back."

"I can't."

Luke stared at Nancy, his face growing increasingly unhappy.

"Could you at least call Ava's date and ask him to call me?" Nancy asked at last.

"Are these two things connected?" he asked.

"What things?" Nancy stalled.

Luke squared his shoulders, and Nancy could

see that she had lost his sympathy. "I'm afraid I can't tell you anything about Ava's date, and I can't even contact him for you. You'll have to speak with her when she returns. Now, if you're not interested in registering for our dating service, I'd like to continue my work."

"If you change your mind, please call me," Nancy said, standing. "I'm in Hartley Hall."

On her way back to the dorm Nancy wondered whether she should have confided in Luke. She had given him barely enough information to make the connection between Ava's absence and her date, and he had jumped quickly to it, which made her suspicious. On the other hand, he seemed unsure and uneasy, as if he was hearing about Ava's disappearance for the first time.

When she got back to the dorm Nancy went to the recreation room to make a call. A large television sat in one corner, and a handful of students lounged on the orange sofas around the room, giving half their attention to the evening news. Nancy settled at one of the two pay phones on the far wall and dialed the Woodses' number.

"It's Nancy Drew," she said when Mr. Woods answered the telephone.

"Nancy!" he said with forced cheerfulness. "I don't suppose you've found Ava yet."

"Not yet, but I'm working on it," she said sympathetically. She filled him in on her actions so far and told him what Betsy had said about Ava's car not being parked on campus.

19

Mrs. Woods, who had picked up on another extension, sucked in her breath. "This really is serious, isn't it?" she said. "Should I call the police about the car?"

"It would be useful to see if they've found it," Nancy said. "I'll give them a call. I won't go into much detail, but if it hasn't turned up, that might tell us something."

Mr. Woods found a copy of the registration and read Nancy the license number. After promising to give them daily reports, Nancy hung up and dialed the police.

"I'm looking for a car," she told the officer. "I'm not sure it was stolen, but it appears to be missing, and I wonder if you have a record of it."

"Appears to be missing?" the man asked skeptically. "Did you lend it to someone?"

"A friend might have borrowed it, but I'm not sure," Nancy said, then gave him the license number and description. She waited, hearing the soft tapping of computer keys as he searched.

"I don't have anything here," he said at last. "When was the last time you saw the car?"

"Friday," Nancy told him. "Could you call me if it turns up?"

"Are you the owner?" he asked. "If it turns up, we'll contact whoever registered the plates."

"Perfect," Nancy said. "Thank you so much."

She headed up the stairs toward her room. As she neared it she saw that the door to Betsy's and

Ava's room was ajar. "Betsy?" Nancy called as she pushed the door open.

The blinds were partly closed. Through the half-light of early evening, Nancy could see that Betsy wasn't in the room.

But someone else was. A young woman with blond hair was seated at Ava's desk, going through her drawers!

Chapter

Three

Nᴀɴᴄʏ ɢᴀꜱᴩᴇᴅ. "Ava?" she asked, flipping on the light. "Is that you?"

The young woman turned, and Nancy saw that she was quite striking, with huge amber eyes and hair like gold. Nancy had never seen her before.

"I was looking for Betsy or Ava," Nancy said. "Am I in the wrong room?"

The blond woman smiled slowly. "I hope not. I was leaving a message for Ava myself." She gestured to the desk. "I was looking for paper."

"I'm Nancy Drew, a friend of Ava," Nancy said, sticking out her hand.

"I'm Maia Edenholm. Ava works for me."

Nancy looked at Maia again. With her long, straight hair and jeans, she could easily have passed as a Halloway student. But up close Nancy could see that she was older, perhaps in her midtwenties.

"She works for you?" Nancy repeated.

"Yes. My fiancé and I run a program for helping elderly people."

"Of course," Nancy said. "The Elderly Assistance program." She paused. "Where's Betsy?"

Maia shrugged. "I haven't seen her. But more to the point, where is Ava?"

"No idea. I just wondered why the door was ajar," Nancy said airily, trying to be vague. "Is there a problem?"

"Only that Ava didn't show up for work today, and my client, Mrs. McCarthy, is screaming about it," Maia said. "Is she sick?"

"I think she took a long weekend," Nancy hedged.

Maia seemed surprised. "Did she tell you that?" At Nancy's curious look, she continued in haste, "She didn't mention it to me or Peter. It's really caused some problems."

"I'm sure she'll clear everything up when she returns," Nancy said mildly.

"Where did she go?" Maia asked.

"She didn't say," Nancy said. "I haven't seen her for several days, though. You didn't have a clue she was leaving?"

"No. It does seem abrupt. Do you think it's suspicious?"

Maia was mimicking Nancy's own style of

answering every question with a question, Nancy realized with surprise. Aloud she said, "Suspicious? For a college student to get away for a few days?"

Maia shrugged. "She always seemed level-headed to me. But if she's this unreliable, maybe it would be better if she stopped working for us."

"Please don't decide that because of what I said," Nancy urged. "I haven't seen her for a while, and I have no idea why she didn't show up for work today."

"My decision is based on Ava, not you," Maia assured her. "My client was very, very upset, and I have to protect her from that. I'm sure you understand." She gave Nancy a frosty smile. "When you see Ava, please tell her we no longer need her at Elderly Assistance."

"I'll tell her to call you," Nancy promised. "I'm sure she'll be very upset about Mrs.— What did you say her name was?"

"McCarthy, Jeanette McCarthy."

"I'll tell her," Nancy said, watching Maia go.

Nancy sat down at Ava's desk, not sure whether to leave the room with the door unlocked. Had Maia been probing for information? she wondered. She could understand why Maia would be upset that Ava didn't show up. Then there was the matter of Mrs. McCarthy. Could she be the woman who'd called Ava?

"There you are!" Nancy recognized Bess's

voice and turned to see her friend standing in the doorway. "I've been running up and down the stairs looking for you. Where have you been?"

"Just wait till I tell you," Nancy said.

"Well, I'm all ears, but mostly I'm all stomach," Bess replied. "The one thing we forgot to get from the dean was meal cards, although from what I've heard, it's just as well. I ordered a pizza, and it ought to be here any minute."

"Great," Nancy said. "All of a sudden I'm starving. I have a problem, though. I'm not sure whether I should leave this room." She told Bess about finding Maia in Ava's and Betsy's room and gave her the highlights of the conversation.

Bess shook her head. "Well, don't worry about the door being open," she said. "If you walk down the hall, you'll see that half the doors are ajar. I guess people don't bother to lock them unless they're leaving the dorm. Betsy's probably in the rec room or something.

"Besides," Bess continued with a superior smile, "the locks are no great security. Have you seen them? Even I could pick something that flimsy, and that's a miracle."

Nancy examined the lock and saw that Bess was right.

"Sit down, Bess. I'm going to use Betsy's phone." She dialed Information, asked for a number for Jeanette McCarthy, and wrote it on a scrap of paper. Then she dialed the number.

"Mrs. McCarthy," she began when an elderly voice answered the telephone, "my name is Nancy Drew, and I'm calling for Ava Woods."

"Yes?"

"This may seem odd, but she asked me to find out if you were trying to reach her."

There was a pause. "Well, not anymore. We were trying to find her this morning. Is Ava there now?" Mrs. McCarthy asked.

"Not right here, no," Nancy said.

"Is she sick? Mr. Hoffs said she was sick."

"She was called away on an emergency, and she won't be back for a few days," Nancy improvised. "She didn't mention anything to you?"

"No, nothing at all, but I guess that's the nature of emergencies, isn't it? Please tell her I hope everything is okay, and I'll see her when she returns."

"Mrs. McCarthy," Nancy continued, "I'm taking messages for Ava, and I wondered if you could help me. A woman called to remind Ava about a box, and she didn't leave her name. Was that you, by any chance?"

"No, I'm sorry. You could try her teachers or her parents," the woman suggested.

Nancy thanked her for her help and hung up.

"You look as if you struck out," Bess said, seeing Nancy's expression.

"Well, Mrs. McCarthy didn't seem desperate to reach Ava, and she said she didn't know anything about a box."

"Time for dinner, then," Bess said happily, tucking her jeans into her boots as she stood. "Why don't I bring the pizza to your room? Mine is a mess."

Nancy agreed. She dashed off a note asking Betsy to call her and begged for five minutes to take a shower. She had just finished dressing when the pizza arrived.

As they ate, Nancy told Bess about her talk with Betsy, and Bess reported on her day.

"I stood in line forever," Bess moaned. "And when I finally got to register, almost all of the classes were filled. I got you into astronomy, which is Ava's class."

"How do you know?"

"The students in each class are listed on the bulletin boards. I had to trade with someone else to get you in. I was almost jealous when I realized you'll have night labs. You'll be gazing at the stars with cute guys."

Nancy sipped her drink. "What did you pick?" she asked.

Bess smiled. "It's a course in myths and legends. I've already learned why people throw rice at weddings."

Nancy raised her eyebrows, and Bess went on. "It was in the course description. People used to throw rocks and twirl knives around the bride and groom to ward off evil spirits. But I guess that was too dangerous, so they changed it to rice."

"See? You're getting something out of school already," Nancy teased.

Bess grabbed a pillow and threatened to throw it. "Your note said you went to Campus Connections. How did it go?"

"I'm not sure," Nancy replied. "The guy who runs it, Luke Jefferies, seemed nervous when I started talking about Ava's date, but I couldn't get him to tell me anything about it."

"Did he tell you who Ava went out with? Any description?"

Nancy shook her head. "He said the information is confidential. Betsy thinks Ava's date's name was Jim and he lives off campus."

"Great. I should be able to date him," Bess said confidently.

Nancy stopped in midbite, and Bess burst out laughing.

"After registration, I couldn't sit around and do nothing," she explained. "So I went to Campus Connections and signed up. I just got back."

"Bess," Nancy cautioned, "we don't know what we're getting into here. Dating this guy Jim could be dangerous—that is, if we ever find him."

"Well, you obviously can't do the dating *and* poke around asking questions. Besides, I'm an expert on guys. I'll find our mystery man if I have to date every one of them on Luke's list."

"I won't let you go alone, Bess. It's too dangerous," Nancy insisted.

"Fine, you can follow me, then, but no interference," Bess warned.

As the two girls cleaned up from dinner, there was a knock on Nancy's door. Maura Parker stuck her head in.

"Just wanted to see how you were getting along," she said with a smile.

Nancy introduced Maura and Bess, and the three girls chatted for a moment. Suddenly another girl appeared in the doorway.

"Maura," the girl said, ignoring Nancy and Bess. "Have you seen Woods today? I'm going crazy trying to find her."

"Good luck," Maura said. "I think she took off again."

"Again!" The girl groaned. "I loaned her a couple of albums. Now I'll never get them back. Let me know if you see her." She walked away.

Nancy turned to Maura. "Are you talking about Ava Woods?" she asked, trying not to seem excited. "I know her from high school. Do you know where she is?"

Maura shook her head. "No, but call her house. Her parents should know."

"I don't think they do," Nancy said casually. "I called them when I got here, and they didn't mention anything."

"They're probably just covering up for her again," Maura said, making a face. "Ava and her mom had another one of their big fights at the end of last week. Ava was yelling loud enough for the whole dorm to hear. Try asking her parents directly. I know they know where she is!"

Chapter

Four

NANCY INVITED MAURA to sit down, and then asked, "Do you remember what Ava was saying when you heard her arguing with her mother?"

"I think she wanted to go to the Mardi Gras in New Orleans, and her parents wouldn't let her," Maura said. "She said she was going anyway. If you know Ava, you know it's not the first time this has happened. Last year it was spring break. Her parents didn't want her to go anywhere, but she took off for Florida. Mrs. Woods called the cops, and Ava was pretty embarrassed when the police tracked her down in Miami."

"That must be why the Woodses didn't want to call the police this time," Nancy said. "Was the fight on Friday?"

"It could have been," Maura said, standing up. "Or maybe it was Thursday. I don't remember. Call the Woodses if you need to know."

"No wonder Betsy was concerned about telling the Woodses that Ava was gone," Nancy said when Maura had left. "Betsy was probably afraid she'd get Ava in trouble."

"But the Woodses didn't mention the fight!" Bess said indignantly. "We could be wasting our time."

"It's true," Nancy admitted. "I wonder why. I'll have to speak to Ava's parents and Betsy tomorrow to see what they're hiding."

Bess stood up and stretched. "Well, this is the shortest mystery we've ever solved. And I was really looking forward to dating all those guys."

"You never know," Nancy said, waving good night. "There may be more here than you think."

Nancy called the Woods residence the next morning, but neither of Ava's parents was at home. She left a message, asking them to call her. Then she looked for Betsy, hoping she could answer a few more questions. But Betsy wasn't around either. Finally, after a quick breakfast with Bess, Nancy decided to go to her astronomy class and see whether she ran into any of Ava's other friends.

When Nancy walked into the classroom she was surprised to see not one but two familiar faces. Darien Olivares and Luke Jefferies were both enrolled in the course.

Darien gave Nancy a delighted smile. She waved weakly in return and took a seat in the back of the room. She hadn't even bothered to get the textbook, she realized. She pulled her notebook out of her bag so she could pretend to take notes.

When she looked up Darien was slipping into a chair beside her.

"Good morning, Nancy," he greeted her warmly. "We meet again, under less violent circumstances."

Nancy smiled despite herself. Darien was trying so hard. "So we do," she agreed. "Are you following me?"

Darien smiled. "I should be," he declared. "We have to pick lab partners, and I was hoping you'd work with me."

Darien is coming on a little too strong, Nancy thought. Why is he so interested in me? "As a matter of fact, I was going to ask Luke Jefferies to be my partner," she said a little coolly.

"You're too late, I'm afraid," Darien said. "He already has a partner."

Nancy looked over and saw that Luke had paired up with a dark-haired girl. In fact, most of the students had chosen partners.

"You're stuck with me, Nancy Drew," Darien said with a laugh. "Don't worry, I'm a good student."

And quite a flirt, Nancy thought to herself, but she allowed him to enter their names as partners on the list when it came around.

The professor began calling off students' names, checking them against the registration list. When he called Ava's name, Luke Jefferies glanced at Nancy, then looked away. He looks unhappy, Nancy noticed. If Ava ran off to Mardi Gras, as Maura thought, why would Luke care?

Nancy turned to Darien. "Ava Woods is a familiar name," she said casually. "I think she lives in Hartley. Do you know her?"

Darien's dark eyes looked amused. He gave Nancy a lazy grin. "I know *of* her."

Nancy tried to draw him out. "I wonder where I could have met her," she said thoughtfully.

"Are you a hockey fan? Ava and that hothead Vince Paratti were quite close for a while."

"Vince Paratti." Nancy pretended to search her memory. "What position does he play?"

"Every Halloway student knows tall, dark, and handsome Vince," Darien said, a challenge in his voice. "He's our temperamental goalie, number one in the league. Who are you kidding?"

"What do you mean?" Nancy asked innocently.

Darien leaned back in his chair, staring steadily at her. "Okay, I'll play your game. Every girl at Halloway is in love with Vince, Nancy. He's dark and dangerous, and he sends shivers up their spines. And you want me to believe you've never even heard of him?"

Nancy shrugged. "I'm not a sports fan," she lied. "Besides, I like blonds."

Darien laughed. "Ooh, that hurt!" he exclaimed.

Nancy ignored him. "Tell me more," she said. "How long ago did Ava and Vince break up?"

Darien shook his head. "You're very good at avoiding questions. I think I'll keep my information to myself. If you want to find out more about Ava Woods, you're not going to find out from me."

"I was asking about Vince, not Ava," Nancy said.

"You were asking about Ava, if I recall," Darien corrected her. "But Vince is a very good place to start."

Darien was being provocative in more ways than one, Nancy realized, surprised. She turned away from him to listen to the professor's lecture. His description of the expanding universe flickered through her mind, but she couldn't concentrate on astronomy.

How did all of the facts fit together? Nancy wondered. Ava's fight with her parents, her blind date, and her hotheaded ex-boyfriend didn't seem to be connected.

Betsy was a mystery, too. She'd never mentioned Vince. She could have forgotten, Nancy supposed, but the combination of two obviously headstrong people seemed interesting, at least. Ava's parents and her roommate all seemed to be hiding something.

Even Darien was not exactly straightforward. Nancy wondered if he knew something about Ava's disappearance. Could that explain his interest in Nancy?

She was itching to leave the lecture and get to work, but she didn't want to arouse Darien's suspicions. First she wanted to talk to the dean about Ava's disappearance during spring break last year. He might also be able to tell her more about Campus Connections and some of the students she'd met.

When the bell rang, signaling the end of class, Nancy hurried to the administration building. Dean Selig had just stepped into a lunch meeting, and his secretary was reluctant to disturb him except for an emergency. Remembering what Betsy had said about Ava's date, Nancy left a note asking the dean for a list of students living off campus, then headed back to the dorm.

Bess was waiting in the lobby. "I got our meal cards," she began, "but judging from that determined look on your face, we won't be eating lunch today."

Nancy grinned. "We'll eat," she assured her friend. Throwing her arm over Bess's shoulder, she guided her upstairs. "Remember the guy who threw the snowball at me yesterday? Well, he was in my class today, and he seems to know more about Ava than he's telling. His name is Darien Olivares. I'm going to see what I can find out about him."

"I could try to date him," Bess offered.

"No. I have someone else for you to date," Nancy replied. "Darien told me Ava has an ex-boyfriend named Vince Paratti. See if Luke has him on a list. He's a hockey player."

"I love athletes," Bess murmured, tossing her blond hair.

"Bess, I don't know what's going on here," Nancy cautioned. "Darien said Vince is a real hothead. It could be a false lead—or he could be dangerous. Try to set up the date, but don't go on it without me."

Nancy and Bess reached the third floor landing. "Let's see what Betsy has to say about Vince and Darien," Nancy suggested. "That way we can at least get started."

Nancy knocked on Betsy's door, but there was no response.

"She's at lunch, I guess," Bess ventured. "Maybe we can catch her in the dining room."

As the two girls debated what to do, the phone in Betsy's room rang.

"Do you think—" Bess began.

"I don't know," Nancy cut in, "but we'd better find out. Do you have a credit card?"

"A meal card!" Bess said gleefully, handing it to her. "Quick!"

Nancy slipped the card into the crack of the door as the phone continued to ring. "Don't hang up," Nancy urged silently as she tried to push the latch back.

The phone stopped ringing, and Nancy heard the click of an answering machine.

"Stay on the phone!" Bess shouted, practically in Nancy's ear. "Leave a message!"

Nancy felt the latch give and pushed the door open. As she reached for the phone she heard an elderly woman's voice on the answering machine.

"Ava? Ava, where are you?"

"Hello?" Nancy said breathlessly into the receiver.

"Ava?"

"No, it's not Ava. I'm a friend of hers," Nancy said. "Who is this, please?"

"I'm looking for Ava. It's very important. Do you know where she is?"

"No, I'm sorry," Nancy began, but the woman interrupted.

"Tell her to call me. She'll know who this is. Please, it's urgent. Just tell her I got a call about the box."

"What box?" Nancy asked quickly.

"The box is the key," the woman said, as if she hadn't heard the question.

Then there was a click, and before Nancy could respond, a dial tone hummed in her ear. The mysterious caller had hung up!

Chapter

Five

Nancy turned to Bess. "This is crazy," she said, shaking her head.

"What's crazy?" Bess asked.

Nancy told her about the conversation she'd just had with the elderly woman. "She said she got a call about the box." Sinking onto Ava's bed, Nancy sighed. "This lady doesn't fit into our picture."

Nancy went through the information she'd collected so far. "Ava is missing," she began. "Her parents asked us to look for her but didn't tell us about a huge fight they had. Betsy reported Ava missing, but she hasn't told us anything else. Luke Jefferies knows something about Ava's date, but he won't tell me about it. Darien is sticking to me like glue, and I think he has something more than flirting in mind. And now we have an elderly woman calling with a desperate message about a box."

"Well, what about that box?" Bess wondered aloud. "Could it be connected to the date? Or to the astronomy course? Darien and Luke are both taking that class."

"I don't see a connection there." Nancy shook her head. "Today was the first class. Which reminds me, we'd better eat before our afternoon classes."

After a quick lunch Nancy checked her schedule and discovered she had several hours before the astronomy lab started.

"I'm going to visit the Elderly Assistance program," she told Bess. "Do me a favor. Call the dean and see if he can tell you anything about Vince Paratti."

"No problem."

Nancy turned back. "And if you can, try to reach Mr. and Mrs. Woods again."

"No problem there, either."

Nancy grinned and hugged her friend. "I know it's more than one favor. You're a lifesaver, Bess. I'm really glad you came."

Bess giggled. "So am I. I've never had a chance to date on the job before."

Nancy set out for the Elderly Assistance office, which she'd found in Ava's address book. She got there in less than ten minutes. It was one of several attached offices in a strip mall in the center of town. Through the display windows, she could see a small reception area decorated in light blue. A sign on the door said Back at Two.

Checking her watch, she saw it was five after two. She pressed the buzzer, but no one answered, so she returned to her car and waited.

After listening to the radio for a few minutes, Nancy saw a car pull up in the space next to hers. Maia Edenholm got out, and then a man stepped out from the driver's side. That must be Peter, the man Maia had mentioned, Nancy decided, the director of the program and Maia's fiancé. She could see flecks of gray in his thick black hair and guessed he was in his early forties. Nancy gave them time to go inside and get settled before she rang the bell.

Maia buzzed Nancy in. From the puzzled look on her face, Nancy could see she was trying to place her. "You're . . ." she began, then stopped.

"Nancy Drew," Nancy said, extending her hand. "We met in Ava Woods's room."

"Of course." Maia's expression shifted to one of alarm. "Did you give Ava my message?"

"Not yet," Nancy said pleasantly. "She hasn't returned."

"I'm glad," Maia said, her face brightening. "Not that she hasn't returned, of course, but that you haven't delivered my message. I'm afraid I was annoyed yesterday. I didn't really mean to fire her. Our clients love Ava. She's welcome to work with us for as long as she wants to."

"Well, I'm sure she'll be delighted to hear that," Nancy said tactfully.

"That couldn't be why you came, though," Maia prompted.

"Well, partly," Nancy said. "But I also want to know more about your program."

"Oh." Maia gave Nancy an appraising look. "Just a sec." She disappeared through a door and reappeared a few minutes later.

"Come on in," she invited.

Nancy walked into a large office. The desk, which dominated the room, was nearly buried under a mess of papers. A key ring the size of a dessert plate was lying near the computer. Books were piled haphazardly on the floor according to size. The man she had just seen outside stepped forward to greet her. He was handsome and tanned, with an easy, athletic gait.

"I'm Peter Hoffs," he said. "Have a seat, and don't mind the mess. It's always like this." His eyes fell on the key ring, and he tossed it at Maia. "Yours," he said. "Put it away."

"Maia said you're Ava's friend," he continued, turning to Nancy. "Any friend of Ava's . . ." He let his voice trail off and gave her a smile. "You know the old cliché. What can I do for you?"

"I met Maia the other day on campus," Nancy

began, feeling her way. "Later I asked around about your program, and everyone had wonderful things to say about it. I thought I'd come by for more information. I was thinking there might be something I could do."

"Sorry, but we don't have any openings," Peter said.

"Oh, I see," Nancy said. "You must have a long list of people waiting to work here."

"We do," he agreed. "I like to think it's because we've got such a good program."

"Well, it can't hurt to hear about the program, anyway, in case you're shorthanded one day," Nancy said.

The phone rang and Maia jumped up. "I'll get it," she volunteered, leaving the room. Peter leaned back in his chair and swung his long legs up onto the desk.

"First thing," he began, "we're not a welfare-type program. Not that there's anything wrong with that, mind you. But our clients are fairly comfortable, financially. They're people who are getting on in age. They have no family nearby to help them, and they need things done now and then."

As Peter continued Nancy could see that those who worked for the program did more than just a few occasional chores. Each assistant, like Ava, visited as many as four clients every week, one each afternoon. They did shopping, housecleaning, and errands. Sometimes they just kept the

43

client company. Peter and Maia also provided professional references, recommending doctors, lawyers, and other specialists when their clients needed them.

Peter's description was smooth and sure, as though he gave it every day. When he finished, Nancy had only two questions.

"Can I ask how much the assistants make?"

"Not much. We pay minimum wage," Peter said. "Our clients aren't rich, you know. We charge just enough to pay our overhead and expenses. I'd love to make the service completely free, but right now we can be charitable only in our feelings."

"And do you organize any help for your clients?" Nancy continued, thinking about Ava's mysterious caller and her reference to a box. "Storage, moving—things like that?"

Peter looked puzzled. "Sure, but most of our clients stay put. And they don't need to store anything, because their families have moved away and left them alone in their houses. If anything, they have too much room."

Nancy smiled and nodded. When she didn't offer anything further, Peter asked, "Is there a special reason you asked?"

"My uncle has a moving company," Nancy fibbed. "I could put you in touch with him if you need something like that. He sells supplies, too: string, tape, plastic covers, boxes. . . ." She let her voice trail off.

Peter Hoffs didn't react to the word "boxes" at all. Checking her watch, Nancy realized her afternoon astronomy lab was scheduled to start soon.

"Well, thank you very much for your time," she said, getting up to leave. "If you do have any openings, even for one day a week, please give me a call. I'd love to help."

Peter Hoffs wrote down her name and the telephone number at the dorm. "I'll call you the minute I need some help," he said, "or a mover."

Nancy got to the astronomy lab a few minutes late. The professor was explaining the parts of a telescope to prepare the class for a visit to the campus observatory.

Luke and his partner were on the other side of the room. Nancy chose an empty seat in the middle of a group, far away from Darien. She wanted to be free to investigate, and she wouldn't be if Darien were at her heels.

The outing to see the telescope would give her a chance to go to the dating service when Luke wasn't there, she realized. But when the professor finally finished his explanation, Darien materialized at her side.

"You didn't sit with me," he teased her. "Has some blond guy stolen you away?"

Nancy winced. "No, actually I was trying to get a job," she said. "Why don't you meet me downstairs? I'll just be a minute."

"I'll wait here," he insisted. "I don't want you to slip out of my sight."

"You want to hang around outside the ladies' room?" she asked with a smile.

Darien blushed. "I'll wait downstairs."

Nancy waited until the class left for the observatory, then headed down the hall in the opposite direction. After finding a back exit, she made her way downstairs. The class was nowhere in sight.

She hopped into her car and drove to Campus Connections. The lobby of the building was quiet and deserted. Nancy pressed the button and waited for an elevator.

She stepped out of the elevator on the third floor. Quickly she took out her lockpick and opened the door to the dating service's offices. Inside, she saw that the door to Luke's office was ajar.

Nancy left the lights off, relying on the afternoon sun coming in through the windows. She turned on Luke's computer, then checked his file drawers but found them locked. Deftly she went through the desk, looking for the keys. It took only a moment to find them.

Now, Nancy thought, satisfied, let's see what's so confidential. She opened the last drawer and pulled out Ava's file.

It contained only a completed questionnaire. Nancy flipped it over to see the evaluation section, but it was blank. She checked for any notes about a date, but there were none. The questionnaire did say Ava liked guys who were tall, dark, and handsome. Just like Darien's description of Vince Paratti, Nancy thought.

Nancy went through a few other files at random. Some contained records of dates, but not many. Either Luke's business wasn't doing as well as he claimed, Nancy thought, or he was terrible at keeping up-to-date records. On a whim, she pulled open the middle drawer and searched through the letter *M*.

"Marvin, Marvin," she muttered under her breath. In a moment she had Bess's file in her hands. Under the question about moonlit walks and nights on the town, Bess had written, "I don't see why you can't have both." Nancy burst out laughing.

According to the questionnaire, Bess's dream date was "an athlete, an intellectual, a lover of movies and the outdoors. But it's the true man inside who makes the date." Nancy had to smile —Bess was certainly covering her bases. There was a date schedule on a second sheet of paper, and Nancy saw that Bess had set up a date with Vince Paratti for the next day. It was lucky he was listed with the service, too, she thought.

Nancy learned two things from the file. First, her friend was really getting into her role as an undercover date! Second, Luke's records for Bess were up-to-date. That could mean someone had removed the record of Ava's date from her file.

Nancy was familiar with the computer program Luke used to keep his records. After checking the menu, she brought up a chronological list of all the Halloway students registered with Campus Connections. Bess's name was close to the bottom.

Right after it, Nancy saw a name that gave her a little chill. Darien Olivares. Was it a coincidence that he'd enrolled in the service right after meeting Nancy? She doubted it.

Nancy asked the computer to search for all first names beginning with *J*, and after a moment, she had three Jims and one James listed on the monitor. She printed the list. As she waited she heard a soft noise in the hall.

She froze. The sound didn't repeat itself. Quickly she grabbed the paper from the printer, folded it, and tucked it into her purse. Still no sound, but as she paused, she thought she heard the door to the outer office open.

Was the lab over already? she wondered. She cleared the screen she had just printed and looked around. There was nowhere to hide. Deciding to talk her way out, she opened the door to Luke's office and stuck her head out.

There was a movement to Nancy's right. As she turned she caught the outline of a figure against the wall in the afternoon light. Before she could get a good look, it swung something toward her. She felt a sharp pain on the back of her head.

I'm falling, she realized hazily. Then she collapsed on the floor.

A dull throb brought Nancy back to consciousness. She lay absolutely still for a moment, trying to remember where she was. Someone had hit her. She could feel a knot at the base of her skull.

There was no sound in the room. Trying to ignore the pounding in her head, Nancy opened her eyes slowly. She was staring at the carpet in the Campus Connections outer office. So far, so good, she thought. She hadn't been moved.

She heard the elevator door open. Get up, she urged herself, lifting her head. Someone's coming. She pushed herself up onto her elbows.

The sight that greeted her eyes wiped every other thought from her head. Luke Jefferies was lying in front of her, blood soaking his shirt.

Nancy gasped in horror as she took in his immobile form. Trying not to panic, she bent over him and checked his pulse. Nothing.

"Police! Freeze!"

At the sound of the deep voice behind her, Nancy whirled around to see four uniformed officers burst into the room. Their guns were drawn, and they were pointing straight at her.

Chapter

Six

NANCY FOUGHT BACK the wave of dread that washed over her. All four officers were staring at her as if she were a murderer. Even through the fog of pain in her head she realized how the scene must appear to them.

"Get up slowly. And keep your hands where we can see them," ordered one of the officers, a stocky lieutenant with short, dark hair.

Nancy obeyed. The pain was drumming through her head, making it hard for her to concentrate.

"Is he dead?" she asked as another officer checked Luke Jefferies's pulse. When the officer nodded, the sick feeling grew in Nancy's stomach.

At the stocky lieutenant's instructions, she put her hands against the wall while he searched her. Luke was dead. The thought kept running through her mind, making her feel queasier and queasier.

"My head," Nancy finally managed to say. "I know what this must look like—"

"Save it," the lieutenant said gruffly. He examined the bump on her head but continued to act wary of her.

"She's clean," he informed the other three officers, who were searching through the Campus Connections office. "Mendez, Mullens, seal off and search the rest of the building. Greer, you continue going through this mess."

Then the lieutenant turned back to Nancy, a hard look in his eyes. She answered truthfully when he asked her her name and what she was doing in Luke Jefferies's office, but he didn't seem convinced by her explanation about investigating Ava Woods's disappearance.

"Just because we haven't found the murder weapon doesn't mean I'm not on to you," he told her. "Now, if you'll come with me to the station, I'm sure the captain will have some questions for you."

Nancy thought of protesting, but she knew it would only look worse for her if she didn't cooperate. Nodding, she followed the lieutenant from the office.

Nancy looked around and noticed for the first

time that someone had ransacked Luke's office. Papers and files littered the floor. The desk was overturned, and the computer was smashed. Nancy wondered if the list she had printed was still in her purse, but she didn't want to draw unnecessary attention to herself by checking.

She barely noticed the commotion outside as the officer led her to a squad car. Several people were milling around, giving the police statements. She'd hear it all later, she thought groggily.

She had to fight to keep her eyes open during the ride to the station. The pounding in her head had lessened somewhat, but it still ached. After a while—Nancy didn't know if it was minutes or an hour—they arrived at the station, and the lieutenant took her to a small room and left her there alone.

She waited quietly until the lieutenant who'd brought her in came back, accompanied by a woman who introduced herself as Captain Vivienne Miller, chief of police.

"It appears you've been very busy at Halloway College, Ms. Drew," Captain Miller began. "Lieutenant Callahan here spoke to Dean Robert Selig, who informed us you're a detective."

Nancy nodded. "A friend of the family is missing, and I offered to help."

"Did you kill Luke Jefferies?" the captain asked, her eyes boring into Nancy.

Nancy put her hand to her head. "I didn't kill anyone. I was looking for something in Luke's office. I heard a noise, and when I went to check someone hit me. Luke was lying next to me when I woke up."

"Luke was there, shot dead," the captain amended. "How do you explain that?"

Nancy spoke very slowly, trying to recreate the situation in her mind. "I don't have a gun. I never use them."

The captain looked at Nancy dubiously. "Several people heard a gunshot, the wound was fresh, and you were the only other person found on the scene. No one else was seen entering or leaving the building."

"It must have happened while I was knocked out," Nancy insisted. "What about the gun? Has it been found?"

Captain Miller exchanged a look with Lieutenant Callahan before answering. "We haven't found the murder weapon—yet," she admitted.

"Am I being charged?" Nancy asked. "If I am, I demand to call my lawyer right away."

The captain looked uncomfortable. "I'm not charging you yet," she said. "But I am interested in learning everything you know about what happened to Luke Jefferies."

Nancy took a deep breath, then launched into her explanation. She told them about Ava's disappearance and how Luke had refused to tell her about the date. Frowning, she tried to remember the few leads she had. When she mentioned reporting the missing car, the lieutenant slipped out of the room—to check her story, Nancy guessed.

Captain Miller asked Nancy to describe her final visit to Campus Connections several times. Nancy gave her Ava's parents' names and telephone number. At last the captain told Nancy she was going to speak with the officers on the scene and left her alone in the room.

It seemed like forever before Captain Miller returned. "I've checked out your story, Nancy," she said. "As I told you earlier, we're not going to charge you. But you're a material witness, and that means you can't leave the area. It also means you stay away from anything to do with Luke Jefferies or Ava Woods."

Nancy shook her head. "I was asked to find Ava, and I'm going to find her. You can't tell me not to. She's my job, not yours."

Captain Miller's eyes blazed for a moment. "Ava *is* my job, Nancy. Craig and Jocelyn Woods have turned the investigation over to the police." Seeing Nancy's disbelief, she continued. "I'm warning you. Stay away from anything that has anything to do with Luke Jefferies and Ava Woods. This is not a game."

Nancy stared steadily at the woman. "I know it's not," she said softly. "I saw Luke, too."

Captain Miller returned her gaze. Finally she

said, "All right, you can go. But if you think of anything else, let us know immediately."

As Nancy walked back to the front desk she saw that the police precinct was packed with people. She asked the desk sergeant if there was a telephone nearby that she could use to call a cab.

"Nancy!" a voice called. Nancy turned to see Darien Olivares. "What are you doing here?"

"Darien!" Nancy said, startled. He was showing up everywhere. "I could ask you the same thing."

"I'm helping the police with their investigation," Darien replied. "But I'm done now. Did I hear you say you need a ride? I was just about to head back to campus."

"Helping the police?" Nancy repeated.

"They're questioning people in the astronomy class, since we were the last ones to see Luke alive."

Nancy didn't see anyone else from the class in the waiting area, but it couldn't hurt to catch a ride, she thought. "Could you pull your car up front?" she asked. "I don't think I can walk very far."

When Darien had disappeared, Nancy turned to the desk sergeant. "Is he helping you with the Jefferies murder?" she asked urgently.

The officer shrugged. "It's none of your business, but I've never seen him before."

Nancy heard a car horn and went to the door. Darien revved his engine as she came out.

"So what were you really doing at the police station?" Nancy asked, putting her seat belt on.

"I told you. Helping the police."

"How did they find you so fast? No one else from class was at the station."

Darien looked uncomfortable. "I was going to Campus Connections to find out about a date."

"You use Campus Connections?" Nancy asked.

"Oh, sure, all the time," he said. "I've met a lot of great people through it."

I'll bet, Nancy thought, remembering when Darien had signed up. One day was hardly enough time to meet a lot of people.

"Darien, stop lying," she said, closing her eyes. "You weren't going to set up a date. Class wasn't over. Neither you nor Luke should have been anywhere near Campus Connections."

Darien stared at the road.

"I hope you don't lie like this to the police," Nancy continued, trying to goad him into answering her. "If you do, they'll start thinking *you* killed Luke."

"Me?" He blanched. "I was outside the whole time!"

"Were you following Luke, or were you following me?" Nancy asked.

"Do you want a ride or not?" Darien said in anger. "If you do, stop accusing me of murder."

They drove the rest of the way in silence. Nancy thanked Darien briefly when they pulled up to Hartley Hall. Stepping out of the car, she realized she was feeling a little better.

Bess had left a message for her at the front desk: "Come to my room immediately!"

With her last bit of energy, Nancy dragged herself to her friend's door.

"There you are!" Bess exclaimed. "The disappearing Nancy Drew. You won't believe the excitement around here. Where have you been?"

"At the police station," Nancy replied, lowering herself onto Bess's bed.

"You look exhausted, poor thing," Bess said, bouncing onto the bed next to her. "Well, if you were at the station, you may have heard the news. Luke Jefferies was murdered."

Nancy sighed. "I know. I'm the number one suspect."

"What?" Bess cried, astounded. "Why?"

"Because I was there when the police found his body." Nancy closed her eyes, trying to keep her head from spinning. "Someone knocked me out. When I woke up I had a lump on the back of my head, and Luke was right next to me—dead."

Bess gave a little shriek. "Oh, no! What happened? Why didn't you call me?" She checked Nancy's head and made her lie down on the bed to tell the story.

When Nancy was finished Bess gave a sympathetic groan. "And I thought you had missed all the excitement," she said. "It must have been awful for you. Are you sure you're okay?"

"I'm fine," Nancy said. "Just tired."

"Do you want me to sleep in your room? You know, in case you feel sick or need anything?"

"No, really, I'm fine. How was your day?"

Bess beamed. "Well, I made a date with Vince Paratti for tomorrow night."

"I saw that when I was at Campus Connections," Nancy said, trying to hide her smile. "Oh, and I have a list of all the Jims registered with the service." She pulled the list from her purse and showed it to Bess.

"Great. I'll date them all," Bess said with satisfaction.

"Bess!" Nancy groaned as she sat up. "Someone was killed today. We have to be very careful. Don't go on any dates without me."

"Don't worry," Bess said. "Now, do you want me to help you to your room?"

Nancy shook her head and said good night. I'm almost in bed, she told herself encouragingly as she climbed the stairs.

From the end of the hall she could see something under her door. It was a plain white envelope. She picked it up, unlocked her door, and collapsed onto her bed. After switching on the light, she slit the envelope open with a fingernail. Suddenly her head began to pound again.

Inside was a short typed message. It read: "Transfer back to wherever you came from, Nancy Drew. What happened to Jefferies could happen to you!"

Chapter

Seven

WHOEVER WAS THREATENING HER hadn't taken the time to push the note all the way into her room, Nancy realized immediately. Dragging herself off the bed, she looked around quickly to see if anything had been disturbed. Finding nothing, she sat back down.

After the day's awful events, the note didn't really scare her. The killer had left her alive this long, so there was a good chance she was safe for the night. Nancy threw the note on her desk with a grim smile. She wasn't always this casual about warnings, she thought as she slipped into her nightshirt and crawled under the covers, but right now she had to get some sleep.

* * *

When Nancy awoke, someone was knocking insistently on her door.

"Are you okay?" Bess asked worriedly when Nancy finally opened the door. "I came by your room once already, but there was no answer."

"Um, I'm fine, I think," Nancy murmured. She felt the back of her head. "My headache is gone. I guess I was just sleeping pretty soundly."

"I'll say. It's after ten o'clock. I was worried about you. Are you going to make it to class today?"

"I don't have time," Nancy replied. "Officially, we're off the case. Mr. and Mrs. Woods handed it over to the police last night. So now we have to move a little more quickly."

"Maybe we should let the police handle it," Bess suggested in a small voice.

Nancy shook her head. "I can't. Ava could be in real trouble, and the police know even less about the case than we do. We still have some leads we need to follow up. Vince, for one. Our list of Jims, for another. And I got a note last night, warning me off the case. That's got to mean I'm getting close to something."

Bess groaned as Nancy handed the warning to her. "All right, count me in," she said.

Nancy thought for a moment. "When's your date with Vince?"

"Tonight. Six o'clock."

"Why don't you drop by the Elderly Assistance program this afternoon?" Nancy suggested. "See if you can get a job. I'll meet you back here at about five."

"Okay," Bess agreed slowly. "You're going to be careful, though, right?"

Nancy shooed Bess out the door, then went down to the pay phones and called Ava's parents. When Mrs. Woods heard Nancy's voice she began to apologize for the ordeal Nancy had gone through the night before. Nancy cut her off gently and asked whether she and her husband could come to the dorm. Mrs. Woods promised that they would get there as soon as they could.

Nancy went back to her room, grabbed a towel, and went down the hall to take a shower. As the hot water drummed on the back of her neck, she sighed, feeling energy seep back into her body.

She was dressed and ready when Ava's parents showed up. After hearing the page, she went downstairs to the lobby to meet them.

Mr. and Mrs. Woods were perched on a sofa, looking uncomfortable. When she saw Nancy on the stairs, Mrs. Woods jumped up and ran over.

"How are you, dear?" she asked anxiously. "The police captain said you'd been hit on the head. We were very worried."

"I'm fine." Nancy smiled and took a seat across from the sofa. "It was just a bump. I want to talk to you about something else, though. I heard you turned the investigation over to the police."

"Oh, Nancy, don't take it badly. Captain Mill-

er insisted. There's a murderer on the loose."
Nancy heard Mrs. Woods's voice falter. "I'm
terrified for Ava," she confessed.

"There's still reason to hope," Nancy said.
"Why didn't you tell me Ava wanted to go to
Mardi Gras?"

Mr. Woods coughed and looked away from
Nancy.

"Well," his wife said, her face red, "we weren't
sure it was connected. And Ava would be furious
if she knew we asked the police or you to look for
her at Mardi Gras. Ava can be impulsive, but we
didn't know she'd just take off like this. We
thought maybe you could figure out where she
went."

Nancy nodded. "But now that there's been a
murder, you're going to let the police handle the
case."

"We can't let you get hurt," Mr. Woods said.
"We'd never forgive ourselves."

"I'd like to keep looking into this on my own,"
Nancy said. "I think I have some leads."

Mr. Woods shook his head. "Hand them over
to the police. I don't want you in any trouble."

"I'll be careful," Nancy insisted. "I want to
check out a few things, and I have an advantage
over the police, because I look like a student.
Besides, the more people we have helping, the
faster we'll find Ava."

Mrs. Woods turned to her husband. "Craig?"
she asked. "What she says makes sense."

"All right," Mr. Woods said at last. "But don't put yourself at any risk. I mean it."

Ava's parents didn't have any more to tell Nancy about Ava's friends or her date. They traded promises to call the minute they heard something. Then Nancy saw them to their car.

When they were gone Nancy reviewed her plans. Betsy was in class, so her first target would be Vince, she decided. How was she going to explain her questions? Talking to the off-campus students would be easy—she could say she was doing a survey for Campus Connections. But with Vince, she'd have to do some fast thinking. Unless she came up with a plan on the way.

Nancy had a quick breakfast and headed down to the hockey rink. Practice was just winding up when she got there. She took a seat in the bleachers and waited, admiring the skill and speed of the players on the ice.

Remembering her conversation with Darien, she turned her eyes to the goalie. Covered by a mask and pads, Vince Paratti was an impressive sight. As Nancy watched, one of the other players sent the puck sailing straight toward his face, and he deflected it without flinching. Nerves of steel, Nancy thought. At least in the rink.

The coach signaled the end of practice, and Vince skated lazily toward the side gate, pulling off his mask as he came. He was quite handsome, with dark wavy hair and fine features. Nancy could see why all the girls at school were in love with him.

She jumped up and went over to him as the team headed toward the locker room. "Hi," she said, giving him her best smile. "Can I talk to you a minute?"

Vince stopped and looked at her. His eyes were black and intense. "What about?"

"Hockey," Nancy said, improvising. "My name's Nancy. My, uh, my little brother is thinking of coming here next year, and he wanted me to find out about the team."

Vince wasn't responding to her charm. She could see that. "Ask the coach," he said, starting to move away.

"My brother wants to talk to someone on the team," Nancy said, starting after Vince. "He's a goalie."

"Tell him to call me, then."

"Great!" Nancy said enthusiastically. She could see she was losing him. "What's your name?"

"Vince Paratti."

"You're kidding!" Nancy exclaimed, trying to prolong the conversation. "I know you! I mean, I know all about you. You're Ava's boyfriend. I'm a friend of hers."

"Not a good friend, obviously," he snapped. "I haven't seen Ava in months."

"You know what I mean," Nancy said, trying

to blush. "And, anyway, I thought you saw Ava the other night."

"No such luck," he said. "Look, if your brother wants to talk about hockey, he can give me a call. I'm in a hurry."

Nancy watched as Vince skated off. He was not very friendly, to be sure. But a murderer? Bess might find out more tonight, she decided.

She went back to her car. Checking her lists, she saw that two of the Jims registered with Campus Connections lived off campus. She'd visit them in alphabetical order. Jim Merriman, she said to herself, here I come.

Nancy followed a street map to a run-down town house several miles from the campus. The front door was painted purple. She rang the bell.

A redheaded guy answered the door. He wore a white shirt and baggy jeans.

"Is Jim Merriman here?" Nancy asked politely.

"Jim!" the guy yelled toward a flight of stairs behind him. "Jim, it's for you again."

Nancy stepped inside gingerly and waited. A pleasant-looking guy with light brown hair and green eyes came running down the stairs. "Yes?" he asked, seeing Nancy.

"Could I talk to you a minute?" Nancy asked. "I'm from Campus Connections."

Jim groaned, gesturing for her to follow him into the living room. "Campus Connections," he said unhappily. "Man, I wish I'd never signed up."

"Why?" Nancy asked, sitting on the sofa.

"Well, it's certainly been more trouble than it's worth," he said. "And I never even met anyone I liked."

"What kind of trouble?"

"What kind do you think?" he asked. "You, for one thing."

Nancy thought quickly. She had no idea what he was talking about. "Me?" she asked.

Jim ran his hands through his hair and leaned back. "Let's do this your way," he suggested. "What can I do for you?"

"I wanted to ask you about your dates," Nancy said. "An informal survey. Where you go, whether you see the people again—"

"And where was I on Friday night, right?" he asked playfully. "Did I go out with Ava Woods?"

Nancy struggled to keep her face neutral. "Why do you ask?"

"Because you're late," Jim said with a small smile. "You should have been here an hour ago. But I'll give you the same answers I gave him. No, I never dated Ava Woods. No, I've never met Ava Woods. I was at the dance Friday night, and everybody saw me there. Sorry to disappoint you."

Nancy smiled despite herself. "I'm certainly sorry to bother you," she said, standing. "I didn't realize the police would talk to you, too."

"Wait," Jim said quickly, the humor fading from his face. "The police? What are you talking about? I thought this was some kind of a joke."

Nancy stopped. "It's not a joke. Who came by here?"

"Oh, man," Jim said, shaking his head. "I ditched some friends Friday night, and I thought they set this up. You mean there really is an Ava Woods?"

Nancy nodded. "We're trying to locate her," she said. "Who did you talk to?"

"Some guy. He said he was a reporter. He had, let's see, dark eyes and dark hair."

"What was his name?"

"I don't remember. I don't think I even asked," Jim said. "I thought it was a joke."

"Well, if you remember or you see him, I'd be interested in knowing," Nancy said, jotting down the phone number of the dorm for him. "Were you really at the dance on Friday?"

"Yes, you can check."

Nancy smiled. "Thanks," she said. As she headed back to her car, she wondered who the mysterious reporter was. An awful lot of people had dark hair and dark eyes, including Vince Paratti and Darien Olivares. Nancy had just left Vince. Darien, on the other hand, seemed to be very much interested in Nancy's movements. Could he have questioned Jim?

Nancy went to see the other guy on her list, Jim

Schaberg. He lived in an apartment about a mile away.

The door opened six inches to Nancy's knock. She could see a chain holding the door close to the frame. One blue eye stared at her. "Yes?"

"Jim Schaberg?"

"Yes?"

"My name is Nancy Drew. May I come in?"

The door shut, and Nancy heard him undo the chain. When it reopened, Jim Schaberg stood looking at her suspiciously. He was slender, with a shock of bright blond hair hanging in his face.

"What do you want?"

"I wanted to ask you a question or two about Campus Connections," Nancy began.

Jim's face darkened. "I don't know Ava Woods. I never dated Ava Woods. And if you don't leave immediately, I'm going to call the police." He slammed the door in her face.

Nancy stared at it for a moment, stunned. She knocked again. The door stayed closed.

"Jim?" she called through the door. "Did a reporter come by here?"

"Go away."

"Please," Nancy insisted, "it's important."

She waited, but there was no reply. "What was his name?" she asked, hoping he was still there.

After a moment Jim's voice came back through the door. "It was Fabian, or something like that."

It *was* Darien, she thought. Aloud she called, "Please open the door for one minute."

"I'm calling the police," he responded.

Nancy backed off. Darien had destroyed any chance she had to get information, but he just might know more than she did, she realized. She'd been too busy with Luke and the dating service to worry about Darien. Was he trying to sabotage her efforts? And where was he getting his information?

Nancy headed back to the dorm. She'd missed both breakfast and lunch, and she was starving. The girl on duty in the dorm was reading a newspaper when Nancy walked in. She glanced up casually, then looked harder at Nancy, an odd expression on her face.

"Is something wrong?" Nancy asked.

"You're the one in the *Banner*," the girl said.

"I don't know what you're talking about," Nancy said, shaking her head slightly.

"It's you," the girl insisted. She pointed to a pile of student newspapers near the elevator. "See for yourself."

Nancy walked over to the pile and picked one up. Her stomach sank. "One Dead, One Missing!" the front-page headline screamed.

Nancy's stomach sank even further when she saw the photograph. It was a picture of her being escorted into the police car.

Chapter
Eight

NANCY QUICKLY SCANNED the newspaper story. "On Friday night a sophomore named Ava Woods was spirited away and has not been seen since," the article began. "Only days later the prime suspect lies dead. Halloway finds itself shrouded in danger and mystery, and no one feels safe."

Nancy grimaced and looked at the byline. "By el Espía" was all it said. *Espía* was Spanish for "spy," Nancy knew. Darien the spy, she thought to herself. Darien the reporter. His story about helping the police was a lie, she realized. He must have come to the police station just to talk to her. Had he also snapped her picture? she wondered. And how did he get there so fast?

70

So Darien was tracking her to get a story, Nancy thought, climbing the stairs.

Reaching her room, Nancy scanned the rest of the article. It said the Campus Connections computer had been wiped clean of all information. To her relief, the story didn't mention that Nancy was a detective. Still, with her name and picture plastered all over the paper, it wasn't going to be easy for her to be discreet, she thought, feeling a headache creeping up the back of her neck.

Nancy checked her watch and realized Bess would be back in about an hour, which didn't give her time to do much of anything. She could get in a nap, though. The events of the night before had exhausted her more than she wanted to admit. After kicking off her shoes, she curled up on her bed and closed her eyes.

Bess's knock woke Nancy an hour later. "Coming," she mumbled as she went to the door.

"Nancy!" Bess exclaimed. "Did you sleep all day? Maybe we should take you to the hospital."

"I was just taking a nap," Nancy protested, yawning. "Don't worry, I feel great."

Bess smiled at Nancy's tousled hair. "Well, you don't look great. What did you do today?"

"I talked to two of our Jims, but Darien Olivares got to them first," Nancy said. "Neither one seemed much like a murderer, but then, I haven't had a chance to check their movements on Friday night.

"Oh, and I met your date," Nancy continued. "He's very handsome, but he's not what you'd call outgoing."

"He's handsome?" Bess's eyes gleamed. "That's all that matters. I'm outgoing enough for both of us."

Nancy smiled. "I guess I'd better get dressed for your date," she said, wandering over to her closet. "One small suitcase doesn't give me much of a wardrobe to choose from. How was your day?"

"Boring. Did you know people throughout history have always thought twins were either evil or magic? I learned that in class today. I've always wanted to be a twin."

"Just think, you could go on twice as many dates," Nancy teased.

"Yeah, and I wouldn't have to clean other people's houses for you."

Nancy whirled. "They gave you Ava's job?"

"Yup! I'm an Elderly Assistance assistant," Bess said proudly.

"Why didn't they give it to me?"

"They said something about suddenly having an opening," Bess offered.

"But they told me there was a long waiting list," Nancy said, shaking her head.

"Maybe they thought I could do a better job," Bess suggested with a grin.

"Well, at least one of us is in," Nancy said.

"Talk to the other assistants. Find out what you can about the clients and Ava. See if anyone mentions a box."

"Nancy"—Bess laughed—"I've helped you before. I'm no beginner at this."

Nancy checked herself. "I know, Bess. Sorry. Did you see the *Banner?*"

Bess shook her head, and Nancy handed her the paper. "Oh, you poor thing," Bess wailed as she looked at the picture.

Nancy finished dressing while Bess read the article. She chose black slacks and a bright blue angora sweater that highlighted her eyes. Silver earrings and just a hint of blusher completed the picture, she decided, looking in the mirror. "I feel like a real person again," she declared.

"We're only going to get pizza," Bess said doubtfully, surveying her own jeans and sweater. "Do you think I should have worn something, you know, more glamorous? I already told him what I would be wearing so he would recognize me."

"You look great, Bess. You always do." Nancy guided Bess toward the door. "I'll go first," she said. "I don't want you alone with this guy. When you get there, sit somewhere where I can hear you. And don't leave with him!"

Bess gave Nancy ten minutes to get to the pizza parlor before her. It was just past the edge of campus, so Nancy decided to walk. When she arrived she saw no sign of Vince. The place was large and noisy, though. She'd have to be fairly close to Bess to hear the conversation.

She ordered a soft drink and some spaghetti at the counter, chose a booth, and sat down to wait. When Bess arrived a few minutes later, she ordered a soda, then managed to get a booth nearby, and began waiting.

Vince walked in about fifteen minutes later wearing a sweat suit. Not exactly dressed for a date, Nancy thought. He looked around the room uncertainly and finally saw Bess.

"Bess Marvin?" Nancy heard him ask.

She could see Bess grin. "You must be Vince," she said gaily. "Sit down."

He shifted his feet restlessly. "Listen, I'm sorry to do this to you, but I can't go on a date tonight," he said in a strained voice. "I tried to reach you by phone, but the dorm switchboard said you weren't in your room."

"No, I wasn't," Bess said. "Listen, I ordered a drink. Could you stay for just a minute? I mean, so I don't have to drink it alone?"

"For a minute," he agreed, lowering his large frame into the booth across from Bess. His back was to Nancy.

"Are you okay?" Bess asked him, concerned. "I mean, I don't know you, but you seem a little upset."

"Yeah," Vince said, "I'm not going to be much fun tonight."

Just then a waiter brought Nancy's spaghetti to her and took Bess's soda to the other booth.

"Order a drink, at least," Bess urged. "It won't take long, I promise."

Nancy saw her smile encouragingly, and Vince studied the menu for a moment.

"A cola and some garlic bread," he told the waiter after a moment.

Bess gave him a brilliant smile. "Do you want to tell me about it?" she asked gently.

Vince shrugged. "Tell me about you, instead."

Nancy concentrated on her food while Bess talked about herself. Her light banter made Nancy smile. Bess was describing her travels with Nancy, leaving out the mysteries they solved. Nancy couldn't meet Bess's eyes as she listened to stories about her golden life, ranging from a summer in the Hamptons to a trip to Hawaii.

By the time Nancy finished her meal, Bess and Vince were laughing over the time Bess tried waterskiing. "You're really fun," she heard Vince say. "I'm glad I came, after all."

"I'm glad I made you feel better," Bess said with warmth in her voice. "You looked pretty down when you walked in."

"I was." Vince hesitated. "Don't take this wrong, okay? I just heard a friend of mine is missing. An old girlfriend, actually."

Nancy's ears perked up. Bess didn't miss a beat. "How terrible! What happened?"

"I don't really know," Vince admitted. "I

75

guess she disappeared on Friday, and she hasn't been seen since."

"I'm so sorry," Bess murmured. "No wonder you didn't want to come out."

"It's okay. It was over between us a long time ago. It just feels funny and I . . ." Vince paused.

Nancy saw Bess reach over and touch his hand.

"I want to help, but there's nothing I can do," Vince said. His voice was filled with frustration and pain. "We haven't seen each other in months. I thought of going to the police, but I don't have anything to tell them."

Bess smiled sympathetically. "I know how you feel," she said. "I hope she's okay."

Vince really did seem unhappy, Nancy thought. Even knowing how quickly information flew around Halloway, she doubted he knew who Bess was. If he did, he would have offered an alibi for Friday night. No, he wasn't faking his concern.

Vince began telling Bess about the hockey team. Nancy decided Bess would be safe for a moment and went to the rest room, avoiding her friend's eyes as she walked past their booth. When she returned, Bess and Vince were leaning toward each other, deep in conversation.

A group of six guys had come in while Nancy was gone. They crowded around a small table, chairs cramming the aisle, blocking Nancy's way.

"Excuse me," Nancy said pleasantly, trying to

squeeze past a burly guy in a down jacket. He didn't even look up.

"Excuse me," Nancy repeated, louder.

Bess and Vince glanced in her direction. The guy in front of her raised his head slowly.

"Yeah?" he asked.

"I just need to squeeze by here—" Nancy began. She heard a squeal from Bess and looked over at her friend.

Vince had leapt to his feet, his face dark and furious. In shock, Nancy saw his eyes were trained on her.

In one explosive motion, Vince charged Nancy.

"Murderer!" he growled.

Nancy scrambled back toward the rest room. Vince followed her, pushing easily past the burly guy. He reached Nancy and grabbed her arm. When she tried to twist away, he shoved her against the wall.

Bess screamed as Nancy's head and shoulders hit the wall. Nancy stared at Vince.

He stood over her, one fist poised to strike. "Murderer," he snarled again. His black eyes bored into hers. "You killed her, didn't you? Didn't you?"

Chapter

Nine

BESS THREW HERSELF between Vince and Nancy. "Stop!" she demanded frantically. "Don't hurt her. She didn't do anything to Ava!"

Confusion danced across Vince's face as he looked angrily from Nancy to Bess. "What's going on here? Bess, how do you know this girl? And how do you know Ava's name?"

Before Bess could reply, the manager of the restaurant came over. "I'm calling the police," he warned Vince. "Leave this young lady alone."

Nancy stepped away from Vince. "We don't need the police," she told the manager. "I'm not hurt. It was just a misunderstanding."

"Go ahead and call the police," Vince said darkly. "This girl is a killer."

"She is not a killer," Bess said hotly, grabbing Vince's arm. "And you're lucky she's not pressing charges. Now let's go outside and sort this out."

To Nancy's surprise, Vince followed Bess out the door. Nancy lagged behind, stopping to pay for their meals along the way.

Bess and Vince were seated on a bench in front of the restaurant, talking quietly, when Nancy got outside. "We're still following up leads," Bess was saying, "but I'm sure we'll find her soon." Vince appeared to have calmed down.

When Nancy reached them, Bess explained. "He saw your picture in the *Banner*, Nancy."

Nancy sat down beside Bess. "Maybe you can help us find Ava," she said to Vince. "I know you haven't seen much of her lately, but any information about her personality may help me."

"If I can help, tell me," he said.

"Well, I may call you if I have any questions," Nancy said. "Is that okay?"

Vince nodded, and Nancy stood up to leave.

He turned to Bess. "So our date was a setup? You were just faking when you said all those nice things?" he asked, ignoring Nancy. "You were investigating me?"

Bess smiled. "No, none of it was fake," she said gently. "I think you're very sweet."

Nancy slipped away diplomatically and wandered over to her car. Bess had the car keys, she remembered, so she couldn't even play the radio while she waited.

Bess joined her moments later. "Young love," she sighed, hopping into the car.

"Who's in love?" Nancy asked, starting the car and pulling out of the parking lot.

"For a detective, sometimes you aren't very observant." Bess sighed. "Vince is in love with Ava. I mean, it's obvious. I told him I couldn't stand in their way. By the way, are you okay?"

Nancy nodded. "After a thump on the head, being thrown against a wall is nothing."

"Good," Bess said mischievously. "Can we go get something to eat? All I had was one piece of garlic bread."

Nancy stopped at a deli, and Bess grabbed a sandwich to go. When they got back to the dorm, there was one more surprise in store for Nancy.

Betsy poked her head into the hall when she heard Nancy's key in her door. "Ava got another call," she said. "It's on the answering machine if you want to hear it."

"Another call about the box?" Nancy asked, joining Betsy inside the room.

"No." Betsy shook her head. "Listen."

As the tape spun, Nancy heard a beep and then a voice.

"It's me," the voice began. "I checked the place, and I'm assuming you arranged the switch. Otherwise, we're in trouble. Please call me."

Nancy looked at Betsy. The other girl was obviously just as puzzled as she was. "It sounds like the same woman who called about the box," Nancy said. "What do you think?"

Betsy shrugged. "I can't be sure," she said. "It seems like a long time ago."

"She talked about a switch," Nancy said thoughtfully. "Did Ava switch anything lately?"

"You got me," Betsy said. "This message is even more cryptic than the earlier one."

"It almost sounds as if Ava's mixed up in some secret scheme," Nancy said thoughtfully.

"Ava would never do anything wrong," Betsy declared. "She's a little wild, but she's got a good heart. She's not a criminal."

"No," Nancy said, "but she does disappear every once in a while, doesn't she? Why didn't you tell me she mentioned going to Mardi Gras?"

Betsy looked down. "I figured if her folks didn't tell you, it wasn't my place to. Besides, I just assumed she'd done something like that again, so I wasn't all that worried."

"Well, I'm worried now," Nancy told her. "So please let me know if anything occurs to you." She headed for the door.

The mention of the switch nagged at the edges of Nancy's sleep. Was Ava hiding something? she wondered. If so, did that make her a victim or had she committed a crime?

The next morning Bess and Nancy split up again. Bess's assignment was to set up a date with anyone named Jim who was registered with Campus Connections, regardless of where he lived. She would also try to check the alibis of Jim Merriman and Jim Schaberg. Nancy headed over to the *Banner* offices to have a talk with Darien.

When she asked for him a girl directed her to an office marked Editor-in-Chief. The door was closed. "He's busy," the girl told Nancy, "but not with a story. It's just his girlfriend. Knock if you get tired of waiting."

Darien's office was set slightly apart from the desks in the rest of the room. No one paid any attention to Nancy. Raised voices drifted through the door in waves, and when Nancy moved closer she could make out some of the words.

"You promised you wouldn't do it," a girl's voice said.

A burst of typing from one of the desks drowned out much of Darien's response. Nancy caught the words "didn't do it to hurt you."

It sounded like a very personal conversation. Nancy was torn between giving them privacy and finding out what was going on. Finally she knocked lightly on the door.

"Come in," Darien called irritably.

Nancy opened the door and saw Darien standing with his arms loosely around a girl who stood with her back to Nancy. "I'm sorry," Nancy said immediately. "I didn't mean to disturb you."

Darien gave her a stricken look. "Ah, Nancy," he said helplessly.

At his words, the girl in Darien's arms turned her tearstained face toward Nancy. It was Betsy Campbell! Her jaw fell, and she stepped away from Darien.

The three of them looked at one another in silence for a moment. Slowly Nancy closed the door behind her. "I'd like to talk to both of you," she said in a determined voice.

"Thanks for tipping me off about Vince Paratti," she continued, looking at Darien. "He came at me last night, and he could have hurt me. He thought I killed Ava."

"I told you he had a temper," Darien said, shrugging. "I thought he was a suspect."

"Darien," Betsy said angrily. "It's bad enough that you wrote about this. I can't believe you've been giving Nancy false clues, too."

"I want to get to the bottom of this," Nancy said quietly. "Betsy, you said you hadn't told anyone about Ava being missing."

"I lied," Betsy said. "I told Darien, but I swore him to secrecy once you came."

"News is news," Darien protested. "You can't keep it quiet. It's un-American."

"So you told him about Campus Connections

and the name of Ava's date," Nancy prodded. "You told him I was coming to Halloway, and about the car—"

"What about the car?" Darien cut in.

Betsy shook her head. "When you came, Nancy, I stopped telling him anything. And I made him promise to stay out of it. At first we both figured Ava would come back. Then, when it began to seem serious, Darien decided to investigate. He thought it could be his big break."

"His big break?" Nancy repeated.

"Darien was a summer intern at a paper, the *Boston Record,* and he wants a job there," Betsy said bitterly. "He thinks if he breaks this story, they'll hire him. That's why he's been following you around."

"And that's why you signed up for Campus Connections, then," Nancy said. "Because you thought you could set up a meeting with me."

"Betsy," Darien said, turning her around to face him. "What about the car?"

"Ava's car is missing, that's all," Nancy said.

"What do you mean, missing? I just saw it."

Nancy looked at him sharply. "This is no time for more false leads, Darien."

"It's not a false lead," Darien insisted, excitement creeping into his voice. "I saw Ava's car this morning."

Nancy stood up. "Show me," she said.

He looked at Nancy and Betsy. "Come on. It

was parked in front of the economics building, as it always is."

The three young people dashed out the door and down to the economics building.

"That's it," Betsy said as they approached the parking lot. "I swear it wasn't here before."

Nancy tried the door. "Locked," she said tensely. Rummaging in her purse, she pulled her lockpick out and opened the door in seconds. Gingerly she searched the car but found nothing unusual. The registration card and insurance form she found in the glove compartment confirmed that it was indeed Ava's car.

"Well," Nancy said, withdrawing her head to look at Darien and Betsy, "someone returned the car."

"I don't understand," Betsy said.

"Ava took the car on Friday night," Nancy said. "She could have brought it back herself in the last day or so and then disappeared again. But it's not likely. My guess is that whoever she met that night brought the car back to throw us off the track. Either way, this tells us she's definitely not in New Orleans having a good time right now."

"Please let her be okay," Betsy pleaded in a small voice.

Nancy gave her a sympathetic look. "We'll have to report this to the police. It'll be public knowledge then, Darien, so you can publish it if you have to. I wish you wouldn't, though. If the person who is responsible for all this knows we're getting close, he or she may just carry out the threat on my life."

"Someone threatened your life?" Darien asked, his eyes round.

Nancy could see the shock in his face. "Let's get some lunch and talk," she suggested. "I need to sort this out."

She didn't learn much over lunch. Darien had followed her to Luke's office two days before, but when he saw Luke going in, he waited out front. That was how he'd gotten the picture of her coming out of the building with the police. Nancy asked Darien if he'd seen anyone suspicious following her or Luke into the building or leaving before the police came.

"Well, there were people coming and going, but none of them looked questionable. Of course, if I'd known there was going to be a murder, I would have taken photos of everyone."

"What about Jim Merriman and Jim Schaberg?" Nancy asked.

"Oh, them," Darien said. "Neither of them has anything to do with this. They both have solid alibis.

"I'm sorry I've been screwing up your investigation, Nancy," he added sincerely. "I won't do a thing from now on. If you're as good as everyone claims you are, maybe you'll unravel the case and give me an interview."

When she finished eating, Nancy excused herself to report the discovery of Ava's car to the police. Then she headed up to Bess's room.

"Come in," Bess called. Nancy opened the door and saw Bess was not alone. She was sipping hot chocolate with a chunky girl whom Nancy had never seen before.

"This is Sophie," Bess said. "She works at Elderly Assistance, and she's giving me a quick orientation for the job today. The teakettle is hers," she added, pointing to an electric pot plugged into the corner. "We're having cocoa. Want some?"

"I'd love some if I'm not intruding," Nancy said, smiling at Sophie. "I'm Chris."

Getting up to fill the pot with more water, Bess hid her smile when she heard Nancy's alias.

"You work for Elderly Assistance?" Nancy asked, watching Bess disappear. "It must feel so good to help people like that."

"Uh, sure," Sophie said.

"I know Bess was saying that, anyway," Nancy continued. "She's really looking forward to it. And Ava Woods—do you know Ava?"

"Yes. She dropped out, didn't she?"

Nancy shrugged, thinking of a way to get Sophie to talk more. "I thought she had a fight with—what's the name of the guy who runs that program?"

"Peter?" Sophie's plain face lit up. "Not Peter. He wouldn't fight with anyone."

"You're talking about Peter Hoffs?" Bess

asked, sailing back into the room. "He's really cute. Of course, he would never look at me," she said hastily, glancing at Sophie.

"That's okay," Sophie said, tossing her short brown hair. "Everyone is in love with him."

"Really? What's he like?" Nancy asked.

Sophie smiled, her pale blue eyes taking on some life. "He's just so nice," she said. "So unselfish. He's very intelligent but also outdoorsy. He likes to sail, but he doesn't hunt because he doesn't want to kill animals, you know."

"Gosh, it sounds as if you and Peter are great friends," Nancy said encouragingly.

"Oh, we are," Sophie assured her. "We talk all the time."

"Have you been sailing with him? Have you been to his house?" Nancy continued.

"No, he's a private person," Sophie answered. "He doesn't invite people to his home. He sculpts, too. He made the most beautiful statue once," Sophie continued. "It was a nymph or a water spirit or something. Mrs. Merrick owned a pair of them, but she gave one to her daughter. Peter made a cast of the one she had left and created a new one for her."

"Wow," Bess said.

The girls chatted further, but Sophie didn't say anything more about the program. When they had drained the last of their cocoa, she picked up her electric teakettle and left.

"Chris!" Bess hooted, when Sophie was gone. "I almost called you Nancy about ten times."

"I didn't want Peter Hoffs to connect you with me," Nancy said mildly. "Sophie seems to be close to Peter."

"I think Sophie has an overactive imagination when it comes to Peter. Of course, if he were a little younger, I'd put him on my dating list."

"And how is your dating list?"

"I set up one date," Bess said, rolling her eyes. "This guy is a real big spender. We're going to meet for a soda in the school cafeteria."

"What time? I'll go with you."

"Nancy, we're going to the school cafeteria in broad daylight! I'll be okay. Besides, the guy sounds like a nerd. He studies archaeology or some science."

"Nancy Drew," a voice broke in. With a start, Nancy realized she was being paged over the dorm's loudspeaker. "Nancy Drew, if you're in the building, please return to your room. Nancy Drew, return to your room."

Bess stared at Nancy, her blue eyes open wide. "Sounds bad. Should I come?"

Nancy nodded, and the two girls dashed up the stairs. Several girls were clustered in the hall near her door. But as she and Bess approached, Nancy saw that the girls weren't by her room—they were huddled outside Betsy's door. Nancy pushed through the crowd and stopped short. The room had been ransacked!

Chapter
Ten

BETSY WAS HUDDLED on her bed with Maura Parker, who had one arm around the frightened girl. Nancy went over to ask what had happened.

"Oh, Nancy!" Betsy said, wiping her eyes. "I just got back, and this is what I found."

"The campus police are coming," Maura said quickly. "I talked to the girl on duty downstairs at the desk, and she doesn't remember any suspicious-looking strangers coming in. I'm not sure what to do."

"Maybe you should ask the girls in the hall to go back to their rooms," Bess suggested. "The quieter we can keep this, the better." Maura got up and went into the hall.

Betsy looked at Bess for a moment. "Who are you?"

"This is Bess Marvin," Nancy explained in a low voice. "She came with me."

"I thought you were alone," Betsy said.

"Bess and I split up so people wouldn't connect us. That way we can cover more ground," Nancy said. "Bess, you'd better go to your job. Doesn't it start soon?"

"Oh, gosh, yes!" Bess checked her watch. "I'm going to meet this guy in the cafeteria afterward. Don't worry," she said, seeing that Nancy was about to protest. "If you don't see me by five, call out the National Guard."

Bess left just as two campus police officers arrived. One checked the door while the other questioned Betsy.

Nancy sat patiently through the questions, only half listening to the answers. No, Betsy said, she didn't know who broke into the room. No, she didn't have any enemies. As far as she could tell, nothing was missing.

Nancy watched as one of the officers checked around the room.

"Excuse me," she said to him. "I noticed you were checking the door. Is the lock broken?"

The officer shook his head. "Looks fine to me. I assumed the door was open."

"No, I locked it," Betsy said.

Nancy's ears perked up at that. The door had been locked, but of course someone could have

91

picked the lock. The other possibility was that whoever had broken in had a key—which meant the intruder probably had Ava!

"Well, we can have someone change the lock, if you'd like," the officer said.

"Thank you," Betsy agreed. "I'd feel safer."

After the men left, Nancy picked up Ava's things and put them away according to Betsy's directions. The two girls went through the mess on Ava's desk together, but Betsy could find nothing missing.

"Did Ava have any hiding places?" Nancy asked in frustration. "The burglar must have come looking for something."

"I'm thinking," Betsy murmured. "Her address book is here; she didn't keep a diary; there wasn't anything hidden in any of her books. . . . Wait a second," she said thoughtfully. "Ava's textbooks aren't here."

"Why would she take textbooks on a date?" Nancy asked.

"She wouldn't. She keeps them in a backpack."

"It wasn't in the car," Nancy said.

"She's got a locker in the gym," Betsy said. "She's not a real athlete, but she plays tennis in the spring and summer. We could try there."

"Great," Nancy said. "Do you know which locker is hers?"

"Number forty-five," Betsy said. "Vince Paratti's hockey number."

"What about the lock?"

"It's a combo lock. I don't know the combination."

"I can't pick a combination lock," Nancy said. "Would she have the number written down anywhere?"

"I doubt it. Ava has a terrific memory. Wait," Betsy said excitedly. "I bet Vince knows the number."

Betsy quickly got Vince on the telephone. He told her he had the number in the gym, and he'd meet them there in a few minutes.

When Nancy and Betsy got to the gym, they found Vince in front of Ava's locker.

"Vince," Betsy said warmly. "It's been a while. You've been avoiding me."

Vince blushed. "No, I haven't," he protested. "I just never see you around."

"I always thought you and Ava would get back together," Betsy continued, ignoring Vince's discomfort. "I guess I underestimated how headstrong you two are."

"Betsy, all that is history," he replied. "Let me open this locker in peace."

Betsy turned to Nancy. "They were together for a year," she explained. "I don't even remember what they fought about, but I do know it was something stupid."

"It wasn't stupid!" Vince protested.

"Then what was it?" Betsy challenged.

"I don't remember," he muttered. "There, the locker's open. Now stop bothering me."

"Vince, she's missing," Betsy said softly. "When she comes back, don't you think you and Ava should try to forgive each other for whatever it was you can't remember?"

Nancy saw a gleam in Vince's eyes. "If you need anything more, call me," he said gruffly. "I've got to get back to the dorm."

Nancy watched him go. "You were pretty hard on him," she commented. "Have you always been a matchmaker?"

Betsy smiled and nodded. "My matches usually work," she said. "Now let's see what we have here."

The backpack was in the bottom of the locker. Nancy and Betsy sat on a bench and went through it carefully.

Ava's astronomy textbook was in the pack, which proved she'd used it recently. In the front pocket, Nancy found a comb, some change, a pencil, two pens, a key to a safe-deposit box, and a slip of paper. On it was an address Betsy didn't recognize: 555 Pussy Willow Drive.

"It's in town," Betsy offered. "You could check it out. It could be anybody's, though, including one of her clients'."

"I'll check with Bess when she comes back," Nancy told her. "I'd like to keep the address, if you don't mind. And the key."

"How do you know it's for a safe-deposit box?" Betsy asked.

"Take a closer look," Nancy said, handing it to Betsy. "Most keys have grooves in their sides, but this one is completely flat."

Betsy flipped it over in her hands. "It doesn't say which bank it's from," she commented.

"Exactly," Nancy said. "That way, the valuables in the box are safer."

When Nancy and Betsy got back to the dorm Bess was in the lobby talking to a young man wearing horn-rimmed glasses. She motioned the two girls over with one hand, a smug expression on her face.

"This is my date, Jim Wilhelm," Bess said proudly. "He just moved off campus about a week ago."

Nancy wondered if the dean hadn't yet found out about Wilhelm's change of address. That could be why Ava's mystery date had been so hard to track down.

"Tell Nancy what you told me, Jim," Bess prompted.

Jim looked uncomfortable. "I don't get it, Bess," he said unhappily. "I never even saw her."

Bess glared at him.

"Okay, okay." He turned to Nancy and Betsy. "I had a date with Ava Woods last Friday night."

"*Had* is the key word," Bess said eagerly. "Luke Jefferies called at the last minute to cancel the date!"

"Luke canceled it?" Nancy asked.

Jim nodded. "He said Ava couldn't come. So I went to the dance instead."

"Then you didn't see her that night?"

Jim shook his head. "Never even met her."

But, Nancy thought, Ava had gone out with someone that night. Luke had switched the dates, and neither Ava nor Jim had been aware of it.

Nancy reviewed the clues carefully. Luke was dead, and the Campus Connections office had been ruined. That told Nancy that Luke wasn't the only person involved in Ava's disappearance. Maybe he had fought with his accomplice. Or Luke could have threatened to expose whatever crime he was mixed up in, and his accomplices could have killed him to keep him quiet. But who was the mastermind—and what was the scam?

After Jim had left, the three girls continued to work on the puzzle.

"Could this be the 'switch' the woman caller was talking about?" Betsy asked.

"I suppose," Nancy said. "But that would mean that Ava was aware of the switched dates. The 'switch' in the telephone call sounded as if Ava had switched something herself.

"Jim's date was canceled so that someone else could meet Ava that night," Nancy continued, ticking off her thoughts on her fingers. "So the mystery date must have known her or known of her."

"And Ava obviously wasn't willing to see

him," Bess joined in. "So he had to trick her into a meeting."

Nancy nodded. "Maybe Luke was just a pawn."

"A dead pawn," Betsy agreed, wincing.

"But why did he go along with it?" Nancy asked. "If only I could talk to him."

She jumped up. "The Campus Connections office is ruined," she said, "and the police have sealed it off. But maybe we can find something in Luke's room."

"But you're a girl," Betsy objected, pointing out the obvious. "It's a boys' dorm. How are you going to get in?"

"I'll sneak in," Nancy said cheerfully. "It's late. There can't be too many people roaming around. But I will need help."

"Maybe Darien could help," Bess suggested, looking to Betsy for her reaction. "He does want to be an investigative reporter, right?"

"He'd love to," Betsy agreed immediately. "It would give him a chance to redeem himself."

"Great," Nancy said. "If we can't get in the front, there has to be a back door."

The girls checked the student directory and found out that Luke had lived in Shafer Hall. Betsy called Darien, who promised to meet Nancy in front of Shafer in ten minutes.

Nancy threw on some baggy jeans and a leather jacket and hid her hair under one of Betsy's hats. When she arrived at the dorm, she found that Darien had already gone to work. "Luke lived on the second floor," he said. "But we can't hang around outside his room too long. There's a police warning on the door, and I'm sure everyone knows which room is his."

"The locks are easy to pick with a credit card," Nancy said, flashing one. "Is there someone on duty in the lobby?"

"Yes, but there's a back entrance that leads directly into the stairwell on the other side of the building. I'll go in the front door and let you in the back way."

Darien disappeared into the dorm, and Nancy walked around to the back. After a few minutes he appeared and unlocked the back door. Nancy stepped in, thinking how simple it was to get inside.

As they crept toward the second floor, Darien said in a low voice, "Luke's room is on the other side of the dorm, so keep your head down."

When they got to the landing, Darien peeked down the hall. "All clear," he reported. "Let me go first and pop the lock. That way you won't be standing in the hall."

Nancy watched him go. He opened the door easily and motioned for Nancy to join him.

Nancy headed down the hall quickly and slipped into Luke's room unseen. She looked around her and shivered. Nothing had been disturbed. A pair of jeans and a sweatshirt were draped over one chair, and his books were scattered around.

Nancy searched Luke's desk and left the rest of the room to Darien. It took about an hour for them to go through everything. At last they had to admit defeat.

"If there was a clue," Darien said, plopping down on a trunk next to the bed, "the police must have removed it."

"Or it's hidden very well," Nancy added.

"What about his gym locker?" Darien wondered.

"What about his mailbox?" Nancy asked, her eyes growing wide.

Darien jumped up. "Ingenious!" he agreed promptly. "It's worth a try. The mailboxes are in the basement."

"Let's go," Nancy said. "We've made it this far."

They listened for sounds in the hall. Hearing only silence, they sneaked out quietly.

To get to the mailboxes, Nancy and Darien had to take the main stairs. Their luck held, and no one saw them slipping down to the basement. Nancy saw the layout was a lot like that of Hartley Hall. The lounge and the kitchen were at the front of the building, and a narrow hallway led to rooms in the back. Mailboxes lined one side of the lounge.

"How do you pick a mailbox lock?" Darien asked.

"It would be easier to pick the lock on the door," Nancy said, gesturing to the little mail room. She pulled out her lockpick. The lock gave easily under her skilled hands.

Inside, Nancy ran her finger over the list of names and pulled the mail from Luke's box. Not even looking to see what was there, she slipped all of his mail inside her leather jacket and joined Darien outside.

They were halfway up the stairs when they heard a voice.

"Hey!" a voice called jokingly. "Girls aren't allowed in this dorm."

"Aw, give us a break," Darien said to the student who had called out. He threw his arm around Nancy and pulled her close. "She was upset, and we really needed a quiet place to talk. But now she feels better, don't you?" he asked, a wicked grin on his face. Quickly he bent and planted a kiss right on Nancy's lips.

"Darien," she warned in a low voice.

"Come on, Nancy," he whispered in her ear, "we're just acting here." Aloud, he said, "See? She's much better."

The guy who called out gave them a conspiratorial smile. "Well, I'm not the head resident, so I don't care," he said. "But you'd better get her out of here fast."

Darien smiled, and he and Nancy ran up the stairs and out the door. They sat on the front steps of Shafer to catch their breath.

"'She was upset'?" Nancy mimicked, raising an eyebrow. "'We really needed a quiet place to talk'? Please!"

"I got us out, didn't I?" he pointed out, grinning. "What's a little lie here and there?"

"You were enjoying yourself a little too much," Nancy said.

"Sorry!" Darien pouted. "No girl has ever complained about my kisses before."

"There's a first time for everything." Nancy laughed and pulled four envelopes out of her jacket. "Let's see what we've got." Sifting through them, she said, "Something from Sears, an offer from a credit card company, a flier for the dance, something from the bursar's office . . ." Nancy opened the last one. "It's a bank statement."

Darien nodded. "There's a student bank on campus," he said. "It's not much, kind of a glorified cash office. But it's hard to get to a bank in town if you don't have a car, so they let us cash checks and make deposits and stuff."

Nancy glanced over Luke's account. Her heart leapt. "Well," she said, "here's something interesting."

Darien peered over her shoulder. "What?"

"It's a deposit for five hundred dollars," Nancy said.

Darien whistled. "That's quite a chunk for a college student."

Nancy turned to him, her eyes shining. "Not only that, look at the date. It was deposited on Friday morning—the day Ava disappeared!"

Chapter

Eleven

Do you think someone paid Luke to get a date with Ava?" Darien asked excitedly.

"It's very possible," Nancy said. Quickly, she filled Darien in on the switched dates. "Five hundred dollars is a lot for a date. That narrows down our suspects quite a bit."

"Do you think someone is planning to hold her for ransom?" Darien asked.

"The Woodses don't have that kind of money," Nancy said. "It's always possible that the money doesn't have anything to do with Ava. Maybe Luke just held on to a bunch of payments and then deposited them all at once."

"I wouldn't keep that much cash lying around,

would you?" Darien said. "Especially since the student bank is open every day."

"I agree with you," Nancy said. "If we're right, then it looks as if Ava was kidnapped."

The next morning, Nancy called Dean Selig.

"Nancy," the dean said heartily when he heard her voice, "what can I do for you? I'm sorry I didn't get back to you the last time you called, but—"

"You've been busy, I know," Nancy supplied.

"Actually, I thought you had dropped the case," the dean said. "This thing with poor Luke Jefferies was so awful, I must say I assumed you'd turned the whole thing over to the police."

"Well, sort of," Nancy said, "but I am still trying to get some information about Luke. In fact, that's why I called."

"Oh. What kind of information?" the dean asked, worry creeping into his voice.

"I need to know about a payment Luke received, and I'm hoping the student bank can help me," Nancy replied. "Instead of having the police come to do an official investigation—you know how disruptive that can be."

Nancy could almost hear the dean nodding on the other end of the telephone line. "I'll call the bursar and tell him you're coming to see him. You'll need access to Luke Jefferies's records, right? Do you have to go back very far?"

"Not far at all," she promised. "I'll be out of there in no time."

Nancy grabbed her notebook and headed down to the bursar's office. When she walked in, a jolly man with glasses greeted her. A bald spot gleamed on top of his head.

"I'm Tom Carroll," he said, ushering Nancy into his office. As he closed his door, he looked around nervously to see if anyone took unusual interest in her. "Dean Selig asked me to show you Luke Jefferies's account," he said in a low voice. "Are you looking for anything in particular?"

"I want to see the recent activity," Nancy said with a small smile, "but I don't need to go back more than a few months. Luke deposited a large sum in the student bank last week, and I thought you might have a record of it."

"Anything recent would be on the computer," the bursar said, walking over to his work station. He typed in Luke Jefferies's name. "How large was the deposit?"

"Five hundred dollars," Nancy said. "Deposited last Friday, I believe."

"Here it is," the bursar said. "It was a cash deposit, not a check."

"Thanks," Nancy said. "Did Luke write any large checks recently, by any chance?"

"No, no checks written," the man said after a moment. "No activity in the last day or so, of course."

"I see," Nancy said. "Is there anything else unusual?"

"Well, he withdrew the amount in person."

"He withdrew the five hundred dollars?" Nancy asked, astonished. "When?"

"On the next business day, which was Monday," the bursar replied. "He didn't even leave it long enough to earn interest."

Nancy's pulse quickened. Monday was the day she had met Luke Jefferies! "He came to the bank in person?" she asked. "Do you know when?"

"The withdrawal was recorded at four o'clock."

Nancy thought hard. She'd seen Luke between two and three that afternoon. That meant he withdrew the money right after their conversation.

Nancy mulled the situation over as she walked back to the dorm. If the money was a payment for switching Ava's date, then maybe Luke got scared and pulled the money out when Nancy began poking around. He wouldn't have been able to hide it, however, because it was already recorded as a deposit. Maybe he went to the kidnapper, threatening to expose the crime. Or he could have tried to give the money back. Whatever he did, Nancy realized grimly, it probably cost him his life.

When she got to her room, she found a note from Bess under her door, asking her to stop by.

Nancy grabbed the slip of paper she had found in Ava's backpack and headed down to Bess's room.

"Hi," Bess said, putting down the romance novel she was reading. "It seemed silly to go to class when there's so much going on. So I thought I'd wait and get an assignment from you."

"What's going on at the Elderly Assistance program?" Nancy asked.

"It's a dead end," Bess complained. "The woman I was supposed to help yesterday wouldn't even let me in! Apparently she dropped out of the program and no one bothered to tell me."

"Dropped out?" Nancy asked quickly. "Why?"

"Her daughter came home," Bess said, "and I guess she didn't want to pay for the program anymore."

"Did she say anything about a box?"

"Of course not," Bess said. "I would have told you right away if she had. Anyway, she wasn't one of Ava's clients, and she doesn't know her."

"So you haven't really begun the program."

"I'm not that lazy," Bess protested. "I went to see another client. We made cookies."

Nancy smiled. "That's not so hard. And?"

"And no boxes. She likes Ava, and she likes Peter and Maia, too. She's not very particular."

"Well, let me know if anything happens today," Nancy said, rising. "Meanwhile, I need a list of places in town that have safe-deposit boxes. Do you want to make some calls?"

"Sure," Bess agreed. "Where are you going?"

"To Pussy Willow Drive," Nancy said.

"What's there?"

"That's what I'm going to find out," Nancy said.

After consulting a map of the town, Nancy drove her blue Mustang slowly through the chilly morning air. Soon she found herself in a beautiful wooded neighborhood. The houses were set on large rolling lawns covered with snow and marked with children's footprints, tire tracks, and other signs of daily living. Not exactly student housing, Nancy thought, checking the mailboxes for names and street numbers.

She missed number 555, even though she was still driving slowly. After backtracking, she saw the problem—there was no house number on the roadside mailbox. She pulled into the driveway and got out in front of a rambling two-story Victorian house with a wraparound porch. She was still looking for the owner's name when she heard footsteps coming to the door.

A bolt slid open, and the door swung wide. Nancy came face-to-face with Maia Edenholm.

Maia was dressed in a stunning strapless evening gown. Her pale skin and bright hair glowed against the blue fabric. A sapphire bracelet hung from her delicate wrist, and her bare feet peeked daintily out from under the dress. Standing there, she reminded Nancy of a fairy-tale princess.

"Hi," Nancy said, admiration in her voice. "You look wonderful. Are you going out?"

"One of these days," Maia said, more to herself than to Nancy. She gave Nancy a half smile. "I'm just trying this dress on for a party we're giving soon. Can I help you?"

"Yes," Nancy said, casting around for a reason for being there. "Remember when I came by the office? I thought your program was terrific."

"Yes?"

"Well, I want to write about it for the school paper," Nancy improvised, borrowing Darien's alibi. "About the importance of helping people and all that. It could help me get a place on the staff. That is, if you don't mind."

Maia seemed amused. "You want to interview me?" she asked.

"Ah, I was hoping to talk to Mr. Hoffs."

"He isn't here right now," Maia told Nancy. "But come on in, anyway."

Nancy walked into a huge living room. An overstuffed couch squatting in front of the large picture window was the only piece of furniture in the room. Through the window she could see a large pond behind the house and a cottage perched along the shore on the other side.

"It's beautiful," she said. "Is all this part of the property?"

"Yeah." Maia crinkled her nose. "It would be nice if we could go skating, but the ice is thin in places. Peter likes it, though. That's his fishing cottage."

"This is a great place for a party," Nancy said, looking around the living room. "There's so much open space."

"You mean, where is all the furniture, don't you?" Maia asked. "We don't like things cluttering the place up. It's too hard to clean.

"Besides," she continued, "we're going on vacation tomorrow for three weeks. I put everything valuable away in case of break-ins."

"Well, it certainly is quite a spectacular house. Is it yours?"

"Oh, no! We could never afford anything like this. It belongs to an old college buddy of Peter's. We're only house-sitting."

"House-sitting?" Nancy asked. "Is the Elderly Assistance program new, then?"

"We've been here a year," Maia said. "We have a long-term lease. Want to see the place?"

"I'd love to," Nancy replied politely.

"I hear Peter is a craftsman," she said casually as they walked through the big house. "Does he have a workroom here?"

"A craftsman?" Maia asked blankly.

Nancy nodded. "Someone told me about a statue he made for one of your clients. It's such an unusual talent."

"Oh, that." Maia dismissed its importance with a wave of her hand. "Who told you that?"

"One of the girls." Nancy pretended not to remember who it was. "Peter has a lot of admirers."

"He sure does," Maia said grimly. "Every time a new girl signs up with the program, we go through the crush stage."

"It must happen with your clients, too," Nancy said.

"The old ladies love Peter," Maia agreed. "But some of the old men think he's a young upstart."

"Well, I'm sure Peter's interest in people is what makes him so good at his job, and he has so much to offer," Nancy said mildly, before changing the subject. "I'm sure Ava Woods loves this house."

"I really don't know what you mean," Maia said, a chill in her voice. "Ava's never been to the house. None of the girls have been here."

"But I got the address from Ava," Nancy said. "I wonder why she had it?"

"Maybe Peter asked her to drop something off," Maia said. "I don't know what you're trying to suggest, but I trust Peter. I can assure you he's not interested in college girls.

"You know, Peter hates publicity," she went on, making it clear that Nancy was no longer welcome. "He says charity is its own reward. I'm sure he'd think your story was a bad idea."

Seeing she would get no further, Nancy thanked Maia for her time and left.

Maia was awfully jealous, Nancy thought as she headed back to the dorm. But somehow she didn't believe Peter Hoffs had swept Ava off her feet and spirited her away. Even if Peter and Ava had a relationship, that wouldn't be a reason for him to kidnap her. And why ransack her room? Why kill Luke Jefferies?

When Nancy got back to Hartley, the girl at the front desk stopped her. "You're Nancy Drew, right? Someone is looking for you—a Bess Marvin. She's called three times in the last ten minutes."

"Did she leave a number?" Nancy asked.

"No, she said she'd just keep trying. I'll page you when she calls again."

Bess must have found something, Nancy realized. "Maybe I'll just sit here for a few minutes," Nancy said. "In case she calls again."

"Good idea," the girl agreed. "She sounded pretty anxious."

Nancy sat in the lobby and tried to read a magazine. Giving up after a page, she went to the bulletin board and stared at the announcements posted there. When the phone rang, she jumped.

"Hartley Hall," the girl at the desk answered promptly. "She's right here." She handed the phone to Nancy.

Through the receiver Nancy heard street

112

noises. "Bess? Are you okay?" She tried to keep the tension out of her voice. "Where are you?"

"I'm better than okay," Bess said eagerly. "You were right about the safe-deposit box!"

"You mean 'the box' is a safe-deposit box?" Nancy asked. "Bess, where are you?"

"I went to help a woman in the program," Bess explained. "And you'll never believe what happened. She gave me an heirloom ring and the key to her safe-deposit box. I'm taking a taxi to the First National Bank to deposit it now."

Chapter

Twelve

Hᴀɴɢ ᴏɴ. I'm coming with you," Nancy said. "What's the address?"

Bess gave it to her and hung up. Nancy took the stairs two at a time and raced down the hall to her room. She grabbed Ava's key and headed down to meet Bess at the First National Bank.

If the key was a clue, Nancy thought, tossing ideas around in her mind, what did it tell her? The key could belong to Ava. That would mean Ava had something in her safe-deposit box—something that someone else wanted badly. Then again, she thought, one of Ava's clients could have lent her the key, as Bess's client had. If so, why did Ava still have it? Had she stolen it?

Or had she stolen something from the client's safe-deposit box? Nancy tried to arrange her thoughts. The phone calls had given her the feeling that Ava was involved in some kind of conspiracy with the woman caller. But what kind of conspiracy?

And how did this fit in with the person who had ransacked Ava's room? It was too big a coincidence if the two weren't connected somehow.

If the kidnapper was looking for the key that Nancy now held in her hand, then Ava was probably still safe. But if the kidnapper was looking for something else, there was a small chance that he or she had found it in Ava's room. Nancy sighed. If that was the case, then Ava was no longer of any use to the person. And since Luke was dead, Nancy was afraid Ava might be, too.

Nancy pulled into the parking lot at the First National Bank. Bess, bundled up in a hat and a down coat, was standing in front of the building, almost dancing with excitement.

"Mrs. O'Connell keeps everything valuable in her safe-deposit box," Bess said in a low voice as the two girls entered the bank. "And guess who told her it was a good idea? Peter Hoffs!"

The two girls approached the bank manager's desk, and Bess held out her key. "Box one forty-three," she said, showing him the key.

"You must be one of the Elderly Assistance girls," the man said. He handed her a logbook. "Sign here, and put EA next to your name."

Bess followed his directions, then filled in the columns for the box number and date as well. When she was done, the manager picked up the logbook.

"I'll be with you in a jiffy," he said, bustling through a door in the back. Returning a moment later, he put the logbook on the counter.

"How did you know I was from Elderly Assistance?" Bess asked.

"Mr. Hoffs advises many of his clients to use our deposit boxes," the manager said. "I've come to expect college-age people to be here for his clients. It's an excellent idea, I must say. Old people are easy prey for burglars."

Nancy looked at the man's name tag. "Excuse me, Mr. Taggert, is this one of your keys?" she asked, holding up Ava's key.

The manager took the key from Nancy's hand. "No," he said, handing it back almost immediately. "The tab is green. That's not ours. Also, the number is too high. We only have about two hundred boxes here. You don't know where it's from?"

"I found it," Nancy explained. "I'm trying to return it to the proper bank."

"Better take it to the police," Mr. Taggert advised. "Someone's going to think you stole it if you keep flashing it around like that."

"Good idea," Nancy said. "But I couldn't get into someone else's safe-deposit box, could I? I thought they were very secure."

"Oh, they are," he said. "You have to have an authorized signature and, of course, the key. Without that, even the owner can't get in."

Nancy nodded. "Who authorizes the signatures?"

"The person who rents the box does. All the EA people have given Peter Hoffs permission to open the boxes. And, of course, you kids can get in, too, once your signature is authorized."

"I haven't had my signature authorized yet, I guess," Nancy said.

"But Miss Marvin has," Mr. Taggert said. "I checked her signature against the signature card in the back. Otherwise I wouldn't be able to let you in."

He pointed toward the vault. "I'll show you the process. Ordinarily, only Miss Marvin would be allowed in the vault. But I'll make an exception for you girls this once."

Mr. Taggert opened the lock on the vault and ushered the girls in. Along two facing walls were rows of small doors in three different sizes—they were the doors to the safe-deposit boxes. A table stood in the center of the vault.

"See, the door to each box has two locks. When you rent a box, you get the key to just one of the locks."

"Does the bank keep a copy of the key?" Nancy asked.

"No," Mr. Taggert replied. "The bank has the key to the second lock only. That way someone from the bank can't open the door unless the box holder—or someone the box holder authorizes —is present."

The bank official held out his hand. "If you give me the key for the box you want, I'll open it for you."

Bess handed him the key for Mrs. O'Connell's box. Mr. Taggert checked the number and located the box. He inserted the key and turned it, then inserted a key of his own in the other lock and turned that, and the small door swung open.

"What happens if I lose the key?" Bess asked as Mr. Taggert drew out a long, narrow metal box and handed it to her.

"Well, we can always drill open the lock, but we'd have to charge you," he answered. "Now, would you like to open that in the private room?"

"What's the private room?" Bess asked.

Mr. Taggert pointed to a closed door on the back wall of the vault. "You can open your box in there. Or, if you like, you can open it on the table here."

"Gee, I don't know," Bess said. "What does Mr. Hoffs do? We want to do the right thing."

Mr. Taggert looked amused. "Mr. Hoffs is a busy man. He doesn't come in here just to drop things off."

"But I thought you said he did," Nancy said.

"I said his signature was authorized. But since you kids are the ones who help these people each day, you're the ones who come in. Mr. Hoffs would have to go see his client, pick up the key, come down here, run the errand, and return the key to the client. He can't always take care of those little details."

"So Mr. Hoffs doesn't have keys to the Elderly Assistance boxes, then?" Nancy asked.

"No, he insists that his clients keep both keys. That way they can be sure no one is poking around in their boxes without their permission."

So Peter couldn't get into the boxes, Nancy thought. They certainly seemed secure.

"I think we'd like to open the box in the other room," Bess said, exchanging a glance with Nancy.

"No problem," Mr. Taggert replied, walking to the door in the rear of the vault and opening it for them. The room beyond was a small cubicle with a ledge on one wall and a chair. Poised above the ledge in one corner was a surveillance camera.

Mr. Taggert saw Nancy looking at the camera as Bess set the box down on the ledge. "Extra security," he said proudly. "Let me know when you're done, ladies."

When Mr. Taggert had left the room, Bess turned to Nancy. "What do you think we'll find?" she asked. "Do you think it's full of treasures?"

"It could be, if Mrs. O'Connell is rich," Nancy offered.

"Or maybe it's empty," Bess continued, her thoughts leaping. "Maybe Peter and Maia got their clients to put all their valuables in one place so they could steal them."

Could that be it? Nancy wondered. She remembered Maia's slinky dress and the expensive-looking bracelet she was wearing when Nancy had stopped by earlier. Maia had said that she and Peter couldn't afford such an extravagant house, but Nancy wondered if they were richer than she claimed.

She shook her head. "Too many missing pieces," she said. "Just open it."

"Okay," Bess said. She lifted the lid and gasped.

"What is it?" Nancy asked. "Is it empty?"

Bess shook her head mutely, and Nancy looked inside. The box was full of cheap-looking jewelry and some yellowing letters from friends—the only treasures in Mrs. O'Connell's life.

The two girls left the bank and went out to the parking lot.

"But I was so sure," Bess said sadly, watching soft snowflakes melt on the windshield of Nancy's Mustang. "If Peter was stealing, Ava could have found out. Then maybe he kidnapped her!"

Nancy nodded. "Part of me agrees with you,"

she said. "But look at the clues. Mr. Taggert said Peter always gives both keys to his clients. If the clients have both keys, how would Peter get into the boxes to steal things? Call his clients up and ask for the keys?"

Bess sighed. "Well, couldn't he just wait until they needed something? Then they'd give one of the assistants their key, and he could take things out of the boxes then."

"Yes, if some of the assistants were helping him do the stealing," Nancy said.

"Right, that could work," Bess brightened. "Maybe Peter tried to get Ava involved, and she threatened to call the police!"

"It's still wrong," Nancy insisted. "Using the students is too chancy. And besides, waiting for his clients to ask for something out of their boxes could take a long time—he couldn't steal everything at once. If he had to wait long enough, some of his clients would find out their things were missing before the others decided to get at theirs. And some of them might never give away their keys."

"He could copy the keys," Bess suggested.

"No, you can't have a safe-deposit box key copied," Nancy corrected. "It's illegal."

"So the box has nothing to do with Ava's disappearance, then?" Bess asked.

But Bess had given Nancy an idea. "Did you get a list of places in town that have safe-deposit boxes?" she asked. She took the list from Bess and whistled. "For a small town, that's a lot of safe-deposit boxes."

"We could split up," Bess offered.

"We only have one key. And besides," Nancy pointed out, "it's getting late. The banks are going to close soon."

"And I thought we were so close! What are we going to do now?"

"We're going to call Betsy," Nancy said. "Keep your fingers crossed that she's in her room. And that Ava has a bank account."

Nancy pulled out of the parking lot and up to a pay phone. She jumped out of the car and ran through the snow to the booth. After dialing Betsy's number, she stood shivering, listening to the rings.

"Hello?" It was Betsy's voice.

"It's me—Nancy. Listen, does Ava have a bank account in town?"

"Yes, she does. What's going on? Where are you calling from?"

"There's no time to explain," Nancy said. "I'm tracing her key, and I've got to get to the bank before it closes."

"It's the Middletown Savings Bank." Betsy gave Nancy the address. "Did you find Ava?"

"No, but I think Peter Hoffs may know where she is," Nancy said grimly.

"Can I meet you somewhere?"

"No, I've got to go. Peter Hoffs and Maia

Edenholm are going on vacation tomorrow. We're running out of time."

"Be careful, Nancy," Betsy pleaded.

Nancy promised and raced back to the car. "The Middletown Savings Bank," Nancy told Bess as they headed out. "My guess is that if Ava needed a bank she could trust, she'd use her own."

"I don't understand," Bess said in a daze. "You think Ava had a safe-deposit box? What for?"

"Well, let's say you're right about the deposit boxes," Nancy began. "Assume Peter Hoffs did kidnap Ava. Then the question is, why?"

"I'm not following you at all," Bess said. "But if Peter kidnapped Ava, it was because she found out he was stealing."

"Why not just kill her? He killed Luke."

Bess frowned. "Because she's no good to him dead?" she asked at last.

"Exactly!" Nancy said pleased. "He needs something. And I suspect that he needs the key I have in my hand. Or rather, he needs whatever the key is hiding. And we're about to find out what it is!"

Chapter
Thirteen

So that means she's still alive," Bess said. "Doesn't it? Hoffs would need Ava to get in."

"I hope so," Nancy replied, searching for the bank along the street.

"But then how do *we* get into Ava's safe-deposit box? The Elderly Assistance program's not going to work here, and Ava's not around to help."

Nancy steered the Mustang into a parking spot in front of Middletown Savings Bank.

"Ava's not here," Nancy said, "but her ID is!" She grabbed her purse and drew Ava's student card out from the bottom. "What do you think?" she asked Bess, holding the card near her face.

Bess bit her lip as she compared the two. "You might pass if they don't pay much attention to your eye color," she said at last. "Why don't you put on my hat?"

Nancy slipped the knit hat over her head and pulled her bangs down straight.

"What about the signature?" Bess asked. "Can you fake it?"

"I'll have to try. Maybe I can say I broke my hand or something."

"I know what you can use," Bess said, turning to look around in the backseat. She handed Nancy a Popsicle stick. "Put it in your glove," she directed. "That way it will look like a splint."

Nancy laughed and did as she was told. "Have you been sneaking ice cream again, Bess?"

"Don't say a word," Bess warned, opening her door. "I saved you again."

As they got out, Nancy checked her watch. "Hurry," she urged, "we only have five minutes before closing."

Nancy and Bess raced up the steps to the bank. Reaching the door, Nancy tugged at her hat, trying to regain her composure. Then they walked up to the bank manager, a young man with an eager smile. The nameplate on his desk read Ryan Gillam.

Nancy put her key on the table. "May I get into my box, please?" She glanced quickly at the key. "It's number two eighty-six."

Ryan picked up the key and handed Nancy a logbook. "Of course," he said. "Please sign here."

Nancy waved her hand, forcing a laugh. "It's not going to be a beautiful signature," she said lightly. "I sprained my finger yesterday, and it hurts like anything."

The bank manager gave her a brief smile but didn't offer any help.

Nancy took the logbook with a sinking feeling in her stomach. Suddenly she couldn't remember what Ava's signature looked like.

"Come *on*, Ava," Bess said. "The bank's about to close!"

"I need a pen," Nancy said, searching her pockets. Her fingers touched Ava's student ID and she pulled it out.

Ava's letters were round and even, she saw with relief. She looked up and saw Ryan Gillam watching her.

"You need this, too, don't you?" Nancy asked, handing him the card. "They always ask for ID."

The bank manager took the card and put it on the desk. Wordlessly he handed her a pen.

Nancy grabbed the pen and scrawled Ava Woods's name in the logbook. Ryan looked at it and gave her a friendly smile. "Let me just check it against your signature card, Miss Woods," he said. "You've got plenty of time to get to your box. We're open until six on Fridays and on Saturday mornings, as well."

As the bank manager disappeared Nancy and Bess traded relieved looks.

"We did it," Bess whispered.

Ryan returned a moment later. "The vault's over here," he said, gesturing Nancy over.

When the door swung open the young man turned to Bess. "Excuse me, but I'm afraid I'll have to ask you to wait outside. Only authorized personnel are allowed inside the vault."

Nancy saw the disappointment clouding Bess's face. "I'll only be a minute," she promised.

The vault looked much like the one at the First National Bank. Ryan Gillam put the safe-deposit box on the table and then walked tactfully back to the door to wait with Bess.

Nancy was surprised to find she was holding her breath. She let it out and unlocked the box, then lifted the lid and pulled out a long velvet case. Carefully she opened it.

It was exactly what she'd suspected! Inside the case a beautiful sapphire necklace lay neatly in a long oval groove. In the center a matching ring sparkled against the midnight black lining. But the clue that pulled the mystery together for Nancy was not in the jewelry case. A smaller groove for a bracelet was molded into the bottom —and it was empty!

Thinking quickly, Nancy slipped the jewelry case inside her jacket. She closed the empty safe-deposit box and locked it.

"I'm finished," she called out.

When the young man returned, Nancy gave him a winning smile. "I really need to open another safe-deposit box. Could you help me?"

The manager looked startled. "Another box?"

Nancy slipped the jewelry case out of her jacket and flashed it at the young man. "I thought this would fit in the other box, but I seem to have filled it. Couldn't we just add a new box onto all the old paperwork?"

"All right," he agreed, puzzled. "Let me just see what's available." He walked past Bess, who was frantically trying to see what was happening from the doorway. A moment later he returned to the vault and pulled another drawer out.

"Put it in here," he directed, unlocking the box itself.

Nancy did as she was told, and moments later the necklace was secure. He handed her the keys.

She didn't take them. "I was hoping I could leave those here overnight," she said. "I'll get the two keys hopelessly confused. Could you do that for me?"

He sighed. "It's very unusual," he said. "But I can hold them. You'll have to sign for them tomorrow. Will you be paying by check?"

"What?"

"The rental fee," Ryan Gillam explained. "Will you pay by check?"

"Oh, right." Nancy followed him out the door. "I'll pay in cash." She ignored Bess's questioning gaze as they went back to the manager's desk. She paid the rent, and Gillam handed her a form to fill out.

Nancy looked at the form and realized she'd never be able to fill it out. She got as far as Ava's name and address.

"My finger really hurts," she complained. "I'm sorry, but it's been bad all day. Could you just copy this information from the other form?"

"Sure, but I'll need your signature again here," the bank manager said, pointing to the bottom of the form.

Nancy signed Ava's name with a flourish and pushed the form across the desk with a promise that she would return the next day for the keys.

The girls left. "You were great in there," Bess crowed as they crossed the parking lot.

"I thought I was caught when he asked me to fill out the form," Nancy said, shaking her head. "It was pure luck."

Bess waited while Nancy unlocked the passenger door. "Okay, I've controlled myself long enough," she said, buckling her seat belt. "What were you doing in there? What did you find?"

Nancy pulled slowly out of the parking space. As she checked the traffic on the road, she told Bess about the necklace and the ring. "They match the bracelet I saw on Maia's wrist this morning," she explained. "I think Maia must have stolen it."

"So Peter and Maia *are* stealing from their clients," Bess said. "But how did the jewels get into Ava's box at the Middletown Savings Bank? Mr. Taggert said Peter Hoffs always uses the First National Bank."

"The jewels must belong to one of Ava's clients," Nancy explained. "Somehow Ava found out the bracelet had been stolen from the set. So she switched the necklace and the ring to a new box in a different bank."

"She switched boxes!" Bess said excitedly. "Of course. That's what the phone calls were all about. The woman wants to know where her jewelry is."

"Bravo, Bess," Nancy said approvingly. "And the calls also mean that Ava checked with the owner of the jewelry before she made the switch. That means she was helping the woman, not stealing the jewelry for herself."

"But wait." Bess stopped. "There's still one thing missing. How did Peter Hoffs get into the boxes?"

"I'm going to test a theory about that." Nancy pulled off the road. "Peter and Maia's house is about a hundred yards up this road. We're going to see if we can find his missing workroom."

Snow was coming down hard as the two girls got out of the car. The late afternoon sun was blocked by the downfall, leaving the sky and the land an indistinct white. The girls darted toward the house, keeping near the trees that lined the property along the road. When they reached the driveway Nancy stopped.

"This is it," she whispered. "The lights are on. We'll have to be careful."

"We're going to break in while they're home?" Bess hissed in alarm.

"No. Maia gave me a tour of the house. The workroom's not there. My guess is it's either in the garage or in a little cottage around back on the other side of the pond. We'll try the garage first. Stay down!" Nancy hissed as they crept toward the house.

There was a door on the side of the garage. Nancy tried the knob. It was unlocked, and the girls hurried inside.

The garage was dark. Nancy switched on a lamp on one of the benches, and the light flared brightly in her face. Quickly she threw her coat over part of the shade, dimming it.

"It's a workroom, all right," Bess observed. "It's filthy."

"You take that side," Nancy said, ignoring Bess's comment, "and I'll look around here. Try not to make any noise."

Peter Hoffs had every imaginable tool, Nancy thought as she inspected her side of the room. Still, the drawers and boxes she searched didn't contain what she was looking for.

"Yuck! I have grease on my jeans," Bess whispered.

"Look in the cupboards," Nancy told her. "I'll search over there." Nancy walked toward Bess and began sifting through some old rags under a table saw. After a while, Bess's voice floated back to her.

"You have to admit, this man is handy," she was saying. "He even makes his own teeth."

Nancy made it to Bess in three steps. "What did you find?" she asked urgently.

"Dental plaster," Bess said, pointing to a container in the cupboard above her head.

"Bess, you're brilliant," Nancy said, trying to remain quiet. She pushed past her and started rummaging through the cupboard.

"What do teeth have to do with jewelry?" Bess whispered.

"Dental plaster is used to make molds of people's teeth. Then the imprint in the mold is used to cast new ones," Nancy explained. Her right hand hit something hard and box-shaped, and she drew it out. It was a block of dental plaster. Searching around, she found two stacks of blocks in the back of the cupboard. "It hardens in about five minutes."

Nancy hurried over to the light. "Remember the statue Sophie mentioned? Peter must have set it in plaster and made a mold of it."

She held the mold under the light. "Look."

"Oh, Nancy," Bess said softly.

Nancy was holding a small piece of pink plaster. In the center was an impression—shaped exactly like a safe-deposit box key!

Chapter

Fourteen

He copies the keys himself!" Bess murmured in awe.

"And he's copied quite a few of them," Nancy observed, going back to the cupboard. "He must have at least thirty molds here."

"We've solved the mystery," Bess said gleefully.

"But we haven't found Ava," Nancy pointed out. "Peter and Maia are about to skip town, and I doubt they're planning to take her home first."

"Are you sure they kidnapped her?" Bess asked. "Maybe she's hiding from them."

Nancy shook her head. "They wouldn't have ransacked her room for the key if she wasn't with them. They can't use it without her." She dug her hands into the pockets of her jeans. "I think Ava's here."

"But where?" Bess asked. "Maia gave you a tour of the house, and she wasn't there, right?"

Nancy gnawed her lip, thinking. "Maybe she's in the fishing cottage," she said at last. "No one would think of going there in the middle of winter. It's a perfect hiding place."

"Right! Oh, poor Ava," Bess said. "I'll bet it's freezing out there."

"Let's just hope she's still alive," Nancy said grimly.

Nancy turned out the light and put on her jacket. Then the two girls ducked quietly out of the garage and ran back into the trees surrounding the house. The sun was almost gone, and the wind had picked up, creating snowdrifts.

"The pond is surrounded by trees," Nancy explained. "Once we get there, we can hide among the trees and no one will see us."

They crept around the back of the house. From where they stood, they could see a long snow-covered hill leading down to the pond.

"There's not a lot of cover here," Nancy admitted. "We'll have to run as fast as we can."

She looked toward the house. She couldn't see any movement through the window. "Now!"

Nancy took off down the hill with Bess right behind her. She could feel her heart pounding in time with her steps. She dared not turn around to see if Peter and Maia had spotted them through the windows. Even if they do, she thought, we'll get to the cottage before they can catch us.

She reached the trees surrounding the pond and grabbed a tree trunk to slow herself down. Bess almost plowed into her as she turned around.

"Ooh," Bess wheezed. "I'm not a runner. Did they see us?"

Nancy looked back at the house. All was quiet. "It looks as if we made it."

Once Bess had caught her breath the two girls began picking their way through the woods toward the cabin. Only the crunch of their feet in the snow marred the silence. Nancy's thoughts were whirling. What if Ava wasn't there? she wondered. Or what if they were too late?

Suddenly Nancy spotted the dark shape of the cabin in front of them. Bess caught up with her.

"I don't see any light," Bess said.

"That doesn't mean anything," Nancy whispered back. "The windows are boarded up, see?"

"What do we do now?"

"Split up, I guess. Look for a way in."

Bess stole away quietly. Inching along, Nancy went the other way. The cottage was rectangular, she saw. There was probably only one door.

Suddenly she heard crashing in the trees.

"Nancy!" a voice called behind her. It was Bess, her voice high and frightened.

Nancy whirled to tell Bess to be quiet.

"Don't move, Nancy," a man's voice warned. With a sinking feeling, Nancy realized that Bess was not alone. Peter Hoffs was with her—and he was holding a gun to her head!

Bess's face was drained and white. "Sorry," she said in a small voice. "He jumped me."

"Put your hands where I can see them, Nancy," Hoffs warned, jerking Bess's arm. "Turn around and move slowly toward the cabin."

Nancy did as she was told.

"Hands on your head," he called from behind her as Nancy stepped into the small clearing around the cottage. "And no heroics or I'll shoot your friend."

Nancy reached the door of the cabin. There was a large iron bar on the outside of the door. Nancy waited for Hoffs and Bess.

Raising his voice, Peter called, "Maia, it's me!" Then he turned to Nancy and ordered her to lift the bolt.

Nancy grasped the heavy bar and shoved it out of the latch. A moment later Maia flung the door open. "Peter!" she exclaimed. "I've been worried sick. . . ." Her voice trailed off as she saw Nancy and Bess. "Oh, no," she moaned.

Peter shoved Nancy hard into the cabin. She stumbled, half falling against a table near the door. A kerosene lantern stood on the floor in the center of the room, sending a dim light flickering along the log walls.

In one corner Nancy saw a girl gagged and

bound to a chair. She was covered with blankets, but Nancy could see a pair of dress pumps sticking out on the floor. Her blond hair was stringy, and her eyes were half closed. Ava Woods! Nancy thought, relief surging through her. Thank goodness she's still alive! But how do I get us out of here?

Peter Hoffs was talking to Maia behind her. "I saw these two girls racing down the hill as if they thought a ghost was chasing them," Nancy heard him say. "So I waited outside and welcomed them personally." He pushed Bess, and Nancy saw her friend hit the rough pine floor beside her. "Tie them up, Maia."

Maia obeyed slowly. "Peter," she said in a low voice as she put Bess in a chair and looped a rope around her wrists, "did you have to bring them here?"

"They were on their way with no help from me," Peter said, waving his gun at Nancy. "Our friend Nancy obviously wasn't interested in the warning note you left in her room, Maia." He waved his gun at Nancy. "Too bad I didn't get rid of you when I eliminated Jefferies," he sneered.

Nodding toward the gun Peter held, Nancy said, "That's the gun you used to kill him, isn't it?"

"It sure is," Peter answered with a smug smile. "But Maia and I will be long gone by the time the police trace anything to me."

Nancy turned as Maia approached her.

"Where am I going to put her?" Maia asked. "There aren't any other chairs."

"Tie her to the bed," Peter said offhandedly.

Nancy scooted over to the bed, watching Maia. Her fairy-tale persona was gone, Nancy saw. She looked more than a little frightened.

Nancy sat on the floor with her feet in front of her as Maia jerked her hands up to the bed frame.

"You're hurting me," Nancy protested.

"Sorry," Maia muttered, but didn't let go of Nancy's hands. Following Peter's instructions, she lashed Nancy's wrists to the springs and brought the rope down to tie her ankles together.

Hoffs leaned against the wall, looking at Nancy with satisfaction. "You thought you were smart," he said. "But look where it got you."

Nancy decided to take a gamble. "Where did it get *you?*" she challenged. "You still don't have the necklace and the ring." Seeing his expression change, she continued, "It's too bad, really. They would have looked beautiful on Maia."

Maia opened her mouth but closed it when she saw Peter's glare.

"We have everything else of value," he said. "I cleaned out all the other boxes. And if it hadn't been for Ava, we'd have the ring and necklace, too." He turned to Maia. "Come on, darling, I think it's time to make our grand exit."

"It's too bad you don't have more time," Nancy commented as Peter and Maia reached the door. "I mean, if *I* could find the jewelry . . ." She let the rest of the sentence dangle.

"You found the necklace and the ring?" Maia asked, greed in her voice. "Where are they?"

Nancy forced herself to laugh. "Do you think I'd tell you? Look at us, Maia. You're leaving us to freeze. In a couple of hours we're all going to be icicles." She could see the conflict in Maia's face. "Go on," she urged the blond woman, "it's a clean getaway. Don't blow it now."

Hoffs strode over to Nancy. He grabbed her jacket, tearing it. "If you're so anxious to freeze, let me help you," he said. Roughly he searched her pockets.

Nancy felt Hoffs's fingers strike the safe-deposit box key in her pocket. Astonishment crossed his face as he pulled it out.

"Maia, I think you have your jewelry," he said with a smirk.

"No, Peter, it's too late," Maia said. "All the banks are closed."

"We could wait," he offered. "There wasn't much in the rest of those boxes. This was going to be our prize."

Maia shook her head. "Someone will be looking for these two," she said, gesturing to Nancy and Bess. "The police would be after us before Monday."

Peter turned to Nancy, fury dancing across his face. "Tell me which bank," he demanded.

Nancy shook her head, putting on a smile.

Enraged, Peter was on her, grabbing her by the throat. "Tell me which bank or you won't have time to become an icicle!" he screamed.

Blackness crept into the edges of Nancy's vision. "Middletown," she gasped. "Middletown Savings Bank."

From the corner, Nancy could hear Ava moan. The sound confirmed Peter's suspicions.

"I'm going down there," he said. "Some banks are open late on Fridays. I'll be back soon."

"You're going to leave me?" Maia asked, dismayed. "Alone?"

"Not alone," he corrected, heading over to Ava. Nancy watched as he untied her. "Stretch your legs, Ava," he invited sarcastically. "You're going to take me to the bank. But remember your friends here. If you try to escape, or even say one wrong word, Maia will kill them."

Nancy looked at Ava standing before her. Tears were slipping silently down the girl's face. Nancy smiled encouragingly at her, hoping Ava would be strong. What is she going to do when Peter finds out I moved the necklace? she thought.

"Watch our little sleuth, Maia," Peter said, handing his fiancée a second gun. "If Ava blows it, she'll see her friends die before her, I promise you that!" Peter shoved Ava out the door, his gun pointed at her back.

The sound of the slamming door echoed in the small cabin. Nancy could hear a scraping noise as

Peter threw the bolt and locked the four of them in. She looked over at Bess, who gave her a lopsided smile. Poor Bess, she was trying so hard to be brave!

Carefully Nancy twisted her wrists, testing the bonds that held her to the bed. The springs creaked softly in the silence of the room, and Maia heard the sound and looked over.

"Just trying to get comfortable," Nancy said.

But the springs had stretched! Nancy thought, a kernel of hope growing in her. If only they didn't squeak, she thought, she might be able to get her hands free.

"Maia," Nancy began, hoping her voice would cover the noise of the uncoiling springs, "does he always lock you in?"

Maia gave Nancy an angry stare. "He does it for my own protection," she explained. "You won't try to attack me if you can't get out."

Nancy sighed. "Why are you doing this? Three murders will be an awful burden for someone so young."

"It wouldn't have been three if you hadn't come poking around," Maia answered in a tight voice. "It wouldn't have been any. We never planned to hurt anyone."

"But you *are* hurting people," Nancy commented.

"And what do you suggest? Should we just let you waltz out the door?"

"Is the jewelry worth it?" Nancy asked.

"As a matter of fact, it is," Maia said angrily. "Maybe you don't know what it's like to be poor, but I do. Those old people lock their stuff up in boxes and don't even know what's in them. I could put it to better use."

"Maia—" Nancy began, but Maia cut her off.

"Just shut up, okay?" she said furiously. "This is your fault. You deserve it!"

"Okay," Nancy said, trying to jerk her wrists free. The ropes were looser, but she needed more time to work on them. She decided to let Maia cool off before she tried to talk again.

Minutes ticked by. Maia began picking at her fingernails nervously, trying not to look at the captive girls. Finally Nancy tried again.

"If I'm going to die anyway," she said, breaking the silence, "at least satisfy my curiosity. Mr. Taggert says Peter never came down to the bank. How did you get into the boxes?"

"I did it," Maia said, boasting. "Taggert thought I was an EA employee. There's a signature on file for me."

"I see. And why return Ava's car?" Nancy asked. "I assume you did that as well."

"We had to get rid of it. And I thought if the police found it on the campus, maybe they would guess Ava had returned after the date."

"You did a lot," Nancy commented. "You must have ransacked Ava's room looking for that key."

Maia nodded. "Everyone thinks I'm a student. No one looks at me twice."

Every time Maia spoke, Nancy twisted her wrists, loosening the ropes and gaining a little more slack. Then suddenly she slipped one wrist out of the bonds. Her hands were free!

"How did you know Ava had discovered your plan?" Nancy asked nonchalantly, letting the blood rush back into her hands. She had to lure Maia over to her somehow so she could grab the gun.

"She called from the bank when she saw the bracelet was missing," Maia replied. "At first she thought the bank was responsible for the theft. Peter told her to bring him the key right away, and I guess that made her suspicious. She refused. He told her he was on his way to the bank to deal with the problem, but by the time he got there, Ava and the jewels were gone.

"Ava hid them in another box somewhere else and wouldn't tell us where they were. Peter even called Mrs. Reeves—the one who owns the jewels—to see if she knew anything. But she played dumb, and he couldn't afford to say too much."

"So when Mrs. Reeves left a message for Ava and said she'd just received a call, she must have meant Peter's call," Nancy said.

Maia's eyes widened. "Mrs. Reeves knows?"

"I don't know how much, but she knows

something," Nancy said. "So Peter arranged to replace Ava's date because she suspected him?"

"That's right," Maia said. "We were afraid she'd go to the police. We had to get her fast."

"So he called Luke Jefferies and paid him to switch Ava's date. But how did he know about the blind date in the first place?"

"She told me about it."

Nancy's mind was working furiously. She needed to fake a medical emergency, she decided. One so quick that no one would have time to think.

"But why did Luke . . ." She stopped in midsentence. Closing her eyes, she stiffened her body suddenly and began to shake, hitting her feet on the floor in a frenzy.

Nancy heard Bess scream. "Help her! Don't just stand there!" She could hear Bess's chair scraping along the floor as she scooted over to Nancy.

"What's going on?" Maia cried, coming toward Nancy. She knelt next to the thrashing girl, trying to hold her steady with one hand. "What's wrong with her?" she asked Bess anxiously.

"She's having a seizure. Do something!" Bess screamed. "Quick!"

Nancy opened her eyes a crack. Maia was frozen in indecision, the gun still in her hand.

She wasn't going to drop it, Nancy realized. It was now or never. In a flash, Nancy exploded toward Maia and dived for the gun!

Chapter

Fifteen

NANCY SLAPPED the gun out of Maia's hand, knocking her over with the force of her charge. Holding the woman facedown on the floor, she warned, "Don't move and I won't hurt you."

The gun had fallen on the bed, and Nancy was still hampered by the bonds on her ankles, but Maia couldn't see that from her position on the floor. "Don't turn around," Nancy said, twisting Maia's arm behind her back. "Get up slowly and untie Bess."

"You're locked in!" Maia protested. "You'll never escape."

Nancy pulled Maia to her knees. "Let me worry about that," she said, pushing Maia toward Bess. "Untie her."

Maia obeyed and freed Bess, who had managed to scoot herself close to Nancy. Nancy kept the pressure on Maia's arm as she directed Bess to untie her feet.

When she was free, Nancy forced Maia into Ava's chair and lashed her hands behind her. She piled the blankets over her but left Maia's mouth free. Then Nancy gestured to the gun on the bed and looked at Maia. "If you try anything, I'll shoot you," she lied. The truth was, Nancy hated the idea of even touching a gun, but Maia didn't have to know that.

Nancy turned to Bess and explained her plan in low tones. "The door swings both ways," she explained. "When he lifts the latch, I'm going to hit him with the door. It should knock him off balance long enough for us to get by."

"Then what?" Bess's voice was hoarse.

"We run like crazy!" Nancy told her. "And hope Ava runs, too. It's not the best plan we've ever had, but at least we have a chance."

The girls didn't have long to wait. When they heard Peter's footsteps, Nancy pretended to reach for the gun, her eyes on Maia. They heard the latch being lifted.

Racing to the door, Nancy shoved it with all her might. The door hit Peter in the face, and he rolled backward into the snow.

"Run!" Nancy yelled as she and Bess flew out of the house. "Ava, follow us!"

Bess raced around the pond, with Nancy behind her. They could hear Maia yelling in the cabin.

Nancy turned. Peter was just getting to his feet. Where was Ava? she thought suddenly. Then, in the gloom of the early evening, she spotted a shadow racing across the ice-covered pond.

"Bess," she called. "Ava's on the pond!"

The two girls watched Ava with dread. She was stumbling, unaccustomed to running after being tied up for so long. Peter Hoffs was on his feet, looking in Ava's direction. Suddenly he took off across the pond after her.

"She can barely run," Bess said desperately. "He's going to catch her."

"Not if we catch him first," Nancy said, sprinting toward the pond.

Bess came after her. "What if we fall through the ice?" she wailed.

"Just don't go near the dark parts where the ice is thin," Nancy puffed. "Stay with me."

Nancy and Bess were gaining on Hoffs, but he was closing in faster on Ava. Ava turned to see where he was and gave a little screech. Stumbling, she kept going for the house.

They were in the middle of the pond. Peter was almost on Ava, and Nancy could see that she'd never make it to the other side.

Hoffs suddenly launched himself at Ava. To Nancy's horror, the two of them went crashing down on the ice. A black hole spread under them, and then Peter and Ava were in the water!

When Nancy and Bess neared the center of the pond, they stopped running and got down on their hands and knees. Nancy crawled toward the middle, Bess behind her. When Nancy got close to the hole in the ice she lay down and inched her way to the edge. Bess lay down behind her and grabbed her legs.

"Ava, quick, grab my hands!" Nancy called, reaching out for her. "You don't have much time."

Nancy thought she could hear sirens in the distance. Not daring to look up, she grabbed one of Ava's hands while Bess held the other. "Back, Bess," she yelled. The two girls inched backward. "Don't struggle," she advised Ava. "We're going to pull you over the lip."

The sound of voices whipped by Nancy as she and Bess pulled Ava slowly out of the water. She grabbed the sobbing girl, trying to warm her with her own body, and looked back toward Hoffs.

The ice was now crowded with people, Nancy saw to her amazement. Two police officers were pulling Peter Hoffs out of the water. And incredibly, Nancy heard a familiar voice. It was Darien!

Nancy looked around at all her new friends. She was seated in front of a roaring fire in the living room of the Woodses' house. Thinking about the events of the night before, she shivered, grateful that everything had turned out all right.

Ava was sitting in an easy chair, drinking hot chocolate, her legs tucked under her like a cat's. Nancy's eyes moved to Darien and Betsy, curled comfortably together on the rug by the hearth. Bess was stretched out near them, waving a marshmallow on a stick near the heat.

"It keeps burning," she complained, glaring at the marshmallow as it turned black.

Ava shivered. "I would have given anything for a nice warm fire last night," she recalled.

Nancy nodded. "It was freezing. I remember looking up and seeing someone bundle you in a blanket and carry you away."

"I would have frozen to death," Ava agreed.

"Well, we might have been able to save you," Nancy said, watching Darien poke the flames. "But Hoffs would have died in that water if it hadn't been for Darien and Betsy."

Betsy made a face. "That man is evil!"

"Well, he and Maia are in custody now," Nancy said. "The police have identified Peter's gun as the one that was used to kill Luke Jefferies. That means that Peter and Maia will be in jail for a long time to come."

"And I got my scoop," Darien said proudly. "On the front page of the city section."

"By el Espía?" Nancy asked wryly.

"By Darien Olivares," Betsy said, smiling, "investigative reporter."

"I never asked you how you knew about the key molds, Nancy," Bess said.

"When I told you that safe-deposit box keys couldn't be copied, it hit me. Peter had a huge ring of keys on his desk the day I went in to see him. I thought, it's *illegal* to copy the keys, but it has to be *possible*. And when I remembered the statue he made, I realized how he'd made the keys."

Nancy smiled to herself. "Speaking of forgetting questions," she said, "I never even asked you how you found us, Darien."

"After you called to ask me about Ava's bank, I was worried," Betsy piped up. "I called Darien, but it took me a while to find him. By the time we finally got to the Middletown Savings Bank, you had already left."

"But we spotted Peter Hoffs coming in," Darien said, taking up the story. "And who was with him but Ava! He looked like a thundercloud, and we didn't dare stop them. But Betsy called the police, and I followed Hoffs and Ava back to his house. I even followed them to the pond, but then I lost them among the trees. So I just waited until I saw Ava again on the ice."

The group fell silent, listening to the fire.

"What's going on here?" Vince Paratti asked, entering the room, a tray of steaming mugs held out before him. "I disappear to help with the dishes and everyone starts moping."

"We're not moping," Darien objected.

"In fact," Ava said, gazing at Vince, "we have a lot to be thankful for."

Vince passed the chocolate around and sat down in front of Ava's chair. "Well, you can be thankful that Nancy and Bess are good detectives —even when they have someone like me messing up their investigation."

"You didn't mess it up," Bess said warmly. "You opened the locker where the key was hidden."

"And I got interrogated by the police," he added. "And I threatened Nancy's life."

"Not seriously," Nancy said. "Darien was the one who messed up my investigation!" Darien, Nancy, and Bess all laughed.

"So Peter killed Luke Jefferies?" Ava ventured in a small voice.

Nancy nodded. "Peter had to keep Luke from telling anyone about switching the dates. I think Luke called him after I visited, to say he knew something fishy was going on and he wouldn't cover up. That must have been why he withdrew the money from the student bank. I think he was going to give the bribe payoff back to Peter."

"I don't know how to thank you," Ava said at last. "Any of you. It was pretty awful." She lowered her eyes and shuddered. "No matter what Peter said, I wouldn't tell him where the key was, because I knew he'd keep me alive only until he had it. I kept praying for someone to find me."

Vince gave Ava a quick hug. "Now you have

someone to keep track of you again," he said softly. "That is, if you want me to."

Nancy saw Ava's face soften as she looked at Vince, tears springing up in her eyes. "I want you to," she whispered.

Darien cleared his throat, embarrassed, and turned to Nancy.

"Why didn't Maia take all the jewelry at once?" he asked. "If she had, none of this ever would have happened."

"I can answer that," Ava said, tearing her eyes from Vince. "Maia wasn't supposed to take the bracelet. Peter was furious about it. He wanted to take everything all at once, at the end, so they wouldn't get caught. But Maia was in love with the jewelry and couldn't resist. So she just took one piece, hoping no one would notice.

"I talked to some of my clients today," Ava continued. "The police visited most of them to let them know that their things are safe. They were so amazed when they heard what happened. And I think they were sad to hear the program had come to an end."

Mrs. Woods came to the door. "It doesn't have to end, sweetheart," she said, perching on the arm of Ava's chair. "I talked to Dean Selig today. He said the Elderly Assistance program could become a campus service."

Ava's face lit up. "What a great idea, Mom!"

"Well, there's a catch," Mrs. Woods said,

smoothing her daughter's hair. "He'll do it only if you promise you'll run it."

Ava hugged her mother. "I'd do it in a minute!" She sat back and surveyed the room. "Of course, I'll need some employees," she said mischievously. Her eyes fell on Bess.

"How about you, Bess?" she teased. "Be my first volunteer. I hear you're great at cleaning."

"No way!" Bess exclaimed. "I know my strengths, and cleaning isn't one of them. But if they need someone to help out at Campus Connections, I'd be glad to—I'm terrific at dating!"

Nancy's next case:

Ned's pal Andrew Lockwood has big plans for the grand old Lakeside Inn. With a little help from his friends, he's going to turn it into the hottest rock club this side of Chicago. But a series of strange and sinister accidents have turned Andrew's design into a blueprint for terror—and someone is bound to get hurt.

The someone is Ned, who falls from a balcony and lands in the hospital. The Lakeside job has turned into a dirty business, and Nancy's determined to clean it up. But digging into the darkest corners of Lakeside Inn's past, she quickly discovers that she may be digging her own grave . . . in *NOBODY'S BUSINESS*, Case #67 in The Nancy Drew Files™.